The author of almost a hundred books and the creator of Jeeves, Blandings Castle, Psmith, Ukridge, Uncle Fred and Mr Mulliner, P.G. Wodehouse was born in 1881 and educated at Dulwich College. After two years with the Hong Kong and Shanghai Bank he became a full-time writer, contributing to a variety of periodicals including *Punch* and the *Globe*. He married in 1914. As well as his novels and short stories, he wrote lyrics for musical comedies with Guy Bolton and Jerome Kern, and at one time had five musicals running simultaneously on Broadway. His time in Hollywood also provided much source material for fiction.

At the age of 93, in the New Year's Honours List of 1975, he received a long-overdue knighthood, only to die on St Valentine's Day some 45 days later.

Some of the P.G. Wodehouse titles to be published by Arrow in 2008

JEEVES

The Inimitable Jeeves
Carry On, Jeeves
Very Good, Jeeves
Thank You, Jeeves
Right Ho, Jeeves
The Code of the Woosters
Joy in the Morning
The Mating Season
Ring for Jeeves
Jeeves and the Feudal Spirit
Jeeves in the Offing
Stiff Upper Lip, Jeeves
Much Obliged, Jeeves
Aunts Aren't Gentlemen

UNCLE FRED

Cocktail Time
Uncle Dynamite

BLANDINGS

Something Fresh
Leave it to Psmith
Summer Lightning
Blandings Castle
Uncle Fred in the Springtime
Full Moon
Pigs Have Wings
Service with a Smile
A Pelican at Blandings

MULLINER

Meet Mr Mulliner
Mulliner Nights
Mr Mulliner Speaking

GOLF

The Clicking of Cuthbert
The Heart of a Goof

OTHERS

Piccadilly Jim
Ukridge
The Luck of the Bodkins
Laughing Gas
A Damsel in Distress
The Small Bachelor
Hot Water
Summer Moonshine
The Adventures of Sally
Money for Nothing
The Girl in Blue
Big Money

P. G. WODEHOUSE

The Clicking of Cuthbert

arrow books

Published by Arrow Books 2008

5 7 9 10 8 6 4

First published in the United Kingdom in 1922 by Herbert Jenkins Ltd

Arrow Books
The Random House Group Limited
20 Vauxhall Bridge Road, London, SW1V 2SA

www.rbooks.co.uk

www.wodehouse.co.uk

Addresses for companies within The Random House Group Limited can be found at: www.randomhouse.co.uk/offices.htm

The Random House Group Limited Reg. No. 954009

A CIP catalogue record for this book is available from the British Library

ISBN 9780099513865

The Random House Group Limited supports The Forest Stewardship Council (FSC), the leading international forest certification organisation. All our titles that are printed on Greenpeace approved FSC certified paper carry the FSC logo. Our paper procurement policy can be found at www.rbooks.co.uk/environment

Typeset by SX Composing DTP, Rayleigh, Essex
Printed and bound in the United Kingdom by
CPI Bookmarque, Croydon, CR0 4TD

The Clicking of Cuthbert

DEDICATION

TO THE
IMMORTAL MEMORY
OF
JOHN HENRIE AND PAT ROGIE
WHO
AT EDINBURGH, IN THE YEAR 1593 A.D.
WERE IMPRISONED FOR
'PLAYING OF THE GOWFF ON THE LINKS
OF LEITH EVERY SABBATH THE TIME OF
THE SERMONSES',
ALSO OF
ROBERT ROBERTSON
WHO GOT IT IN THE NECK IN 1604 A.D.
FOR THE SAME REASON

CONTENTS

FORE!

This book marks an epoch in my literary career. It is written in blood. It is the outpouring of a soul as deeply seared by Fate's unkindness as the pretty on the dog-leg hole of the second nine was ever seared by my iron. It is the work of a very nearly desperate man, an eighteen-handicap man who has got to look extremely slippy if he doesn't want to find himself in the twenties again.

As a writer of light fiction, I have always till now been handicapped by the fact that my disposition was cheerful, my heart intact, and my life unsoured. Handicapped, I say, because the public likes to feel that a writer of farcical stories is piquantly miserable in his private life, and that, if he turns out anything amusing, he does it simply in order to obtain relief from the almost insupportable weight of an existence which he has long since realized to be a wash-out. Well, to-day I am just like that.

Two years ago, I admit, I was a shallow *farceur.* My work lacked depth. I wrote flippantly simply because I was having a thoroughly good time. Then I took up golf, and now I can smile through the tears and laugh, like Figaro, that I may not weep, and generally hold my head up and feel that I am entitled to respect.

If you find anything in this volume that amuses you, kindly bear in mind that it was probably written on my return home after losing three balls in the gorse or breaking the head off a favourite driver: and, with a murmured 'Brave fellow! Brave fellow!' recall the story of the clown jesting while his child lay dying at home. That is all. Thank you for your sympathy. It means more to me than I can say. Do you think that if I tried the square stance for a bit. . . . But, after all, this cannot interest you. Leave me to my misery.

POSTSCRIPT. – In the second chapter I allude to stout Cortes staring at the Pacific. Shortly after the appearance of this narrative in serial form in America, I received an anonymous letter containing the words, 'You big stiff, it wasn't Cortes, it was Balboa.' This, I believe, is historically accurate. On the other hand, if Cortes was good enough for Keats, he is good enough for me. Besides, even if it *was* Balboa, the Pacific was open for being stared at about that time, and I see no reason why Cortes should not have had a look at it as well.

P. G. WODEHOUSE

1 THE CLICKING OF CUTHBERT

The young man came into the smoking-room of the club-house, and flung his bag with a clatter on the floor. He sank moodily into an arm-chair and pressed the bell.

'Waiter!'

'Sir?'

The young man pointed at the bag with every evidence of distaste.

'You may have these clubs,' he said. 'Take them away. If you don't want them yourself, give them to one of the caddies.'

Across the room the Oldest Member gazed at him with a grave sadness through the smoke of his pipe. His eye was deep and dreamy, – the eye of a man who, as the poet says, has seen Golf steadily and seen it whole.

'You are giving up golf?' he said.

He was not altogether unprepared for such an attitude on the young man's part: for from his eyrie on the terrace above the ninth green he had observed him start out on the afternoon's round and had seen him lose a couple of balls in the lake at the second hole after taking seven strokes at the first.

'Yes!' cried the young man fiercely. 'For ever, dammit! Footling game! Blanked infernal fat-headed silly ass of a game! Nothing but a waste of time.'

The Sage winced.

'Don't say that, my boy.'

'But I do say it. What earthly good is golf? Life is stern and life is earnest. We live in a practical age. All round us we see foreign competition making itself unpleasant. And we spend our time playing golf! What do we get out of it? Is golf any *use*? That's what I'm asking you. Can you name me a single case where devotion to this pestilential pastime has done a man any practical good?'

The Sage smiled gently.

'I could name a thousand.'

'One will do.'

'I will select,' said the Sage, 'from the innumerable memories that rush to my mind, the story of Cuthbert Banks.'

'Never heard of him.'

'Be of good cheer,' said the Oldest Member. 'You are going to hear of him now.'

* * * * * * * * *

It was in the picturesque little settlement of Wood Hills (said the Oldest Member) that the incidents occurred which I am about to relate. Even if you have never been in Wood Hills, that suburban paradise is probably familiar to you by name. Situated at a convenient distance from the city, it combines in a notable manner the advantages of town life with the pleasant surroundings and healthful air of the country. Its inhabitants live in commodious houses, standing in their own grounds, and enjoy so many luxuries – such as gravel soil, main drainage, electric light, telephone, baths (h. and c.), and company's own water, that you might be pardoned for imagining life to be so ideal for them that no possible improvement could be added to their lot. Mrs Willoughby Smethurst was under no such delusion. What

Wood Hills needed to make it perfect, she realized, was Culture. Material comforts are all very well, but, if the *summum bonum* is to be achieved, the Soul also demands a look in, and it was Mrs Smethurst's unfaltering resolve that never while she had her strength should the Soul be handed the loser's end. It was her intention to make Wood Hills a centre of all that was most cultivated and refined, and, golly! how she had succeeded. Under her presidency the Wood Hills Literary and Debating Society had tripled its membership.

But there is always a fly in the ointment, a caterpillar in the salad. The local golf club, an institution to which Mrs Smethurst strongly objected, had also tripled its membership; and the division of the community into two rival camps, the Golfers and the Cultured, had become more marked than ever. This division, always acute, had attained now to the dimensions of a Schism. The rival sects treated one another with a cold hostility.

Unfortunate episodes came to widen the breach. Mrs Smethurst's house adjoined the links, standing to the right of the fourth tee: and, as the Literary Society was in the habit of entertaining visiting lecturers, many a golfer had foozled his drive owing to sudden loud outbursts of applause coinciding with his down-swing. And not long before this story opens a sliced ball, whizzing in at the open window, had come within an ace of incapacitating Raymond Parsloe Devine, the rising young novelist (who rose at that moment a clear foot and a half) from any further exercise of his art. Two inches, indeed, to the right and Raymond must inevitably have handed in his dinner-pail.

To make matters worse, a ring at the front-door bell followed almost immediately, and the maid ushered in a young man of pleasing appearance in a sweater and baggy knickerbockers who apologetically but firmly insisted on playing his ball where it lay, and what with the shock of the lecturer's narrow escape and the spectacle of the intruder standing on the table and working away with a niblick, the afternoon's session had to be classed as a complete frost. Mr Devine's determination, from which no argument could swerve him, to deliver the rest of his lecture in the coal-cellar gave the meeting a jolt from which it never recovered.

I have dwelt upon this incident, because it was the means of introducing Cuthbert Banks to Mrs Smethurst's niece, Adeline. As Cuthbert, for it was he who had so nearly reduced the muster-roll of rising novelists by one, hopped down from the table after his stroke, he was suddenly aware that a beautiful girl was looking at him intently. As a matter of fact, everyone in the room was looking at him intently, none more so than Raymond Parsloe Devine, but none of the others were beautiful girls. Long as the members of Wood Hills Literary Society were on brain, they were short on looks, and, to Cuthbert's excited eye, Adeline Smethurst stood out like a jewel in a pile of coke.

He had never seen her before, for she had only arrived at her aunt's house on the previous day, but he was perfectly certain that life, even when lived in the midst of gravel soil, main drainage, and company's own water, was going to be a pretty poor affair if he did not see her again. Yes, Cuthbert was in love: and it is interesting to record, as showing the effect of the tender emotion on a man's game, that twenty minutes after he had met Adeline he did the short eleventh in one, and as near as a toucher got a three on the four-hundred-yard twelfth.

I will skip lightly over the intermediate stages of Cuthbert's courtship and come to the moment when – at the annual ball in aid of the local Cottage Hospital, the only occasion during the year on which the lion, so to speak, lay down with the lamb, and the Golfers and the Cultured met on terms of easy comradeship, their differences temporarily laid aside – he proposed to Adeline and was badly stymied.

That fair, soulful girl could not see him with a spy-glass.

'Mr Banks,' she said, 'I will speak frankly.'

'Charge right ahead,' assented Cuthbert.

'Deeply sensible as I am of—'

'I know. Of the honour and the compliment and all that. But, passing lightly over all that guff, what seems to be the trouble? I love you to distraction—'

'Love is not everything.'

'You're wrong,' said Cuthbert, earnestly. 'You're right off it. Love—' And he was about to dilate on the theme when she interrupted him.

'I am a girl of ambition.'

'And very nice, too,' said Cuthbert.

'I am a girl of ambition,' repeated Adeline, 'and I realize that the fulfilment of my ambitions must come through my husband. I am very ordinary myself—'

'What!' cried Cuthbert. 'You ordinary? Why, you are a pearl among women, the queen of your sex. You can't have been looking in a glass lately. You stand alone. Simply alone. You make the rest look like battered repaints.'

'Well,' said Adeline, softening a trifle, 'I believe I am fairly good-looking—'

'Anybody who was content to call you fairly good-looking would describe the Taj Mahal as a pretty nifty tomb.'

'But that is not the point. What I mean is, if I marry a nonentity I shall be a nonentity myself for ever. And I would sooner die than be a nonentity.'

'And, if I follow your reasoning, you think that that lets *me* out?'

'Well, really, Mr Banks, *have* you done anything, or are you likely ever to do anything worth while?'

Cuthbert hesitated.

'It's true,' he said, 'I didn't finish in the first ten in the Open, and I was knocked out in the semi-final of the Amateur, but I won the French Open last year.'

'The – what?'

'The French Open Championship. Golf, you know.'

'Golf! You waste all your time playing golf. I admire a man who is more spiritual, more intellectual.'

A pang of jealousy rent Cuthbert's bosom.

'Like What's-his-name Devine?' he said, sullenly.

'Mr Devine,' replied Adeline, blushing faintly, 'is going to be a great man. Already he has achieved much. The critics say that he is more Russian than any other young English writer.'

'And is that good?'

'Of course it's good.'

'I should have thought the wheeze would be to be more English than any other young English writer.'

'Nonsense! Who wants an English writer to be English? You've got to be Russian or Spanish or something to be a real success. The mantle of the great Russians has descended on Mr Devine.'

'From what I've heard of Russians, I should hate to have that happen to *me*.'

'There is no danger of that,' said Adeline, scornfully.

'Oh! Well, let me tell you that there is a lot more in me than you think.'

'That might easily be so.'

'You think I'm not spiritual and intellectual,' said Cuthbert, deeply moved. 'Very well. Tomorrow I join the Literary Society.'

Even as he spoke the words his leg was itching to kick himself for being such a chump, but the sudden expression of pleasure on Adeline's face soothed him; and he went home that night with the feeling that he had taken on something rather attractive. It was only in the cold, grey light of the morning that he realized what he had let himself in for.

I do not know if you have had any experience of suburban literary societies, but the one that flourished under the eye of Mrs Willoughby Smethurst at Wood Hills was rather more so than the average. With my feeble powers of narrative, I cannot hope to make clear to you all that Cuthbert Banks endured in the next few weeks. And, even if I could, I doubt if I should do so. It is all very well to excite pity and terror, as Aristotle recommends, but there are limits. In the ancient Greek tragedies it was an ironclad rule that all the real rough stuff should take place off-stage, and I shall follow this admirable principle. It will suffice if I say merely that J. Cuthbert Banks had a thin time. After attending eleven debates and fourteen lectures on *vers libre* Poetry, the Seventeenth-Century Essayists, the Neo-Scandinavian Movement in Portuguese Literature, and other subjects of a similar nature, he grew so enfeebled that, on the rare occasions when he had time for a visit to the links, he had to take a full iron for his mashie shots.

It was not simply the oppressive nature of the debates and lectures that sapped his vitality. What really got right in amongst him was the torture of seeing Adeline's adoration of Raymond Parsloe Devine. The man seemed to have made the deepest possible impression upon her plastic emotions. When he spoke, she leaned forward with parted lips and looked at him.

When he was not speaking – which was seldom – she leaned back and looked at him. And when he happened to take the next seat to her, she leaned sideways and looked at him. One glance at Mr Devine would have been more than enough for Cuthbert; but Adeline found him a spectacle that never palled. She could not have gazed at him with a more rapturous intensity if she had been a small child and he a saucer of ice-cream. All this Cuthbert had to witness while still endeavouring to retain the possession of his faculties sufficiently to enable him to duck and back away if somebody suddenly asked him what he thought of the sombre realism of Vladimir Brusiloff. It is little wonder that he tossed in bed, picking at the coverlet, through sleepless nights, and had to have all his waistcoats taken in three inches to keep them from sagging.

This Vladimir Brusiloff to whom I have referred was the famous Russian novelist, and, owing to the fact of his being in the country on a lecturing tour at the moment, there had been something of a boom in his works. The Wood Hills Literary Society had been studying them for weeks, and never since his first entrance into intellectual circles had Cuthbert Banks come nearer to throwing in the towel. Vladimir specialized in grey studies of hopeless misery, where nothing happened till page three hundred and eighty, when the moujik decided to commit suicide. It was tough going for a man whose deepest reading hitherto had been Vardon on the Push-Shot, and there can be no greater proof of the magic of love than the fact that Cuthbert stuck it without a cry. But the strain was terrible, and I am inclined to think that he must have cracked, had it not been for the daily reports in the papers of the internecine strife which was proceeding so briskly in Russia. Cuthbert was an optimist at heart, and it seemed to him that, at the rate at which the inhabitants of that interesting country were murdering one another, the supply of Russian novelists must eventually give out.

One morning, as he tottered down the road for the short walk which was now almost the only exercise to which he was equal, Cuthbert met Adeline. A spasm of anguish flitted through all his nerve-centres as he saw that she was accompanied by Raymond Parsloe Devine.

'Good morning, Mr Banks,' said Adeline.

'Good morning,' said Cuthbert, hollowly.

'Such good news about Vladimir Brusiloff.'

'Dead?' said Cuthbert, with a touch of hope.

'Dead? Of course not. Why should he be? No, Aunt Emily met his manager after his lecture at Queen's Hall yesterday, and he has promised that Mr Brusiloff shall come to her next Wednesday reception.'

'Oh, ah!' said Cuthbert, dully.

'I don't know how she managed it. I think she must have told him that Mr Devine would be there to meet him.'

'But you said he was coming,' argued Cuthbert.

'I shall be very glad,' said Raymond Devine, 'of the opportunity of meeting Brusiloff.'

'I'm sure,' said Adeline, 'he will be very glad of the opportunity of meeting you.'

'Possibly,' said Mr Devine. 'Possibly. Competent critics have said that my work closely resembles that of the great Russian Masters.'

'Your psychology is so deep.'

'Yes, yes.'

'And your atmosphere.'

'Quite.'

Cuthbert in a perfect agony of spirit prepared to withdraw from this love-feast. The sun was shining brightly, but the world was black to him. Birds sang in the tree-tops, but he did not hear them. He might have been a moujik for all the pleasure he found in life.

'You will be there, Mr Banks?' said Adeline, as he turned away.

'Oh, all right,' said Cuthbert.

When Cuthbert had entered the drawing-room on the following Wednesday and had taken his usual place in a distant corner where, while able to feast his gaze on Adeline, he had a sporting chance of being overlooked or mistaken for a piece of furniture, he perceived the great Russian thinker seated in the midst of a circle of admiring females. Raymond Parsloe Devine had not yet arrived.

His first glance at the novelist surprised Cuthbert. Doubtless with the best motives, Vladimir Brusiloff had permitted his face to become almost entirely concealed behind a dense zareba of hair, but his eyes were visible through the undergrowth, and it seemed to Cuthbert that there was an expression in them not unlike that of a cat in a strange backyard surrounded by small boys. The man looked forlorn and hopeless, and Cuthbert wondered whether he had had bad news from home.

This was not the case. The latest news which Vladimir Brusiloff had had from Russia had been particularly cheering. Three of his principal creditors had perished in the last massacre of the *bourgeoisie*, and a man whom he owed for five years for a samovar and a pair of overshoes had fled the country, and had not been heard of since. It was not bad news from home that was depressing Vladimir. What was wrong with him was the fact that this was the eighty-second suburban literary reception he had been compelled to attend since he had landed in the country on his lecturing tour, and he was sick to death of it. When his agent had first suggested the trip, he had signed on the dotted line without an instant's hesitation. Worked out in roubles, the fees offered had seemed just about right. But now, as he peered through the brushwood at the faces round him, and realized that eight out of ten of those present had manuscripts of some sort concealed on their persons, and were only waiting for an opportunity to whip them out and start reading, he wished that he had stayed at his quiet home in Nijni-Novgorod, where the worst thing that could happen to a fellow was a brace of bombs coming in through the window and mixing themselves up with his breakfast egg.

At this point in his meditations he was aware that his hostess was looming up before him with a pale young man in horn-rimmed spectacles at her side. There was in Mrs Smethurst's demeanour something of the unction of the master-of-ceremonies at the big fight who introduces the earnest gentleman who wishes to challenge the winner.

'Oh, Mr Brusiloff,' said Mrs Smethurst, 'I do so want you to meet Mr Raymond Parsloe Devine, whose work I expect you know. He is one of our younger novelists.'

The distinguished visitor peered in a wary and defensive manner through the shrubbery, but did not speak. Inwardly he was thinking how exactly like Mr Devine was to the eighty-one other younger novelists to whom he had been introduced at various hamlets throughout the country. Raymond Parsloe Devine bowed courteously, while Cuthbert, wedged into his corner, glowered at him.

'The critics,' said Mr Devine, 'have been kind enough to say that my poor efforts contain a good deal of the Russian spirit.

I owe much to the great Russians. I have been greatly influenced by Sovietski.'

Down in the forest something stirred. It was Vladimir Brusiloff's mouth opening, as he prepared to speak. He was not a man who prattled readily, especially in a foreign tongue. He gave the impression that each word was excavated from his interior by some up-to-date process of mining. He glared bleakly at Mr Devine, and allowed three words to drop out of him.

'Sovietski no good!'

He paused for a moment, set the machinery working again, and delivered five more at the pit-head.

'I spit me of Sovietski!'

There was a painful sensation. The lot of a popular idol is in many ways an enviable one, but it has the drawback of uncertainty. Here to-day and gone to-morrow. Until this moment Raymond Parsloe Devine's stock had stood at something considerably over par in Wood Hills intellectual circles, but now there was a rapid slump. Hitherto he had been greatly admired for being influenced by Sovietski, but it appeared now that this was not a good thing to be. It was evidently a rotten thing to be. The law could not touch you for being influenced by Sovietski, but there is an ethical as well as a legal code, and this it was obvious that Raymond Parsloe Devine had transgressed. Women drew away from him slightly, holding their skirts. Men looked at him censoriously. Adeline Smethurst started violently, and dropped a tea-cup. And Cuthbert Banks, doing his popular imitation of a sardine in his corner, felt for the first time that life held something of sunshine.

Raymond Parsloe Devine was plainly shaken, but he made an adroit attempt to recover his lost prestige.

'When I say I have been influenced by Sovietski, I mean, of course, that I was once under his spell. A young writer commits many follies. I have long since passed through that phase. The false glamour of Sovietski has ceased to dazzle me. I now belong whole-heartedly to the school of Nastikoff.'

There was a reaction. People nodded at one another sympathetically. After all, we cannot expect old heads on young shoulders, and a lapse at the outset of one's career should not be held against one who has eventually seen the light.

'Nastikoff no good,' said Vladimir Brusiloff, coldly. He paused, listening to the machinery.

'Nastikoff worse than Sovietski.'

He paused again.

'I spit me of Nastikoff!' he said.

This time there was no doubt about it. The bottom had dropped out of the market, and Raymond Parsloe Devine Preferred were down in the cellar with no takers. It was clear to the entire assembled company that they had been all wrong about Raymond Parsloe Devine. They had allowed him to play on their innocence and sell them a pup. They had taken him at his own valuation, and had been cheated into admiring him as a man who amounted to something, and all the while he had belonged to the school of Nastikoff. You never can tell. Mrs Smethurst's guests were well-bred, and there was consequently no violent demonstration, but you could see by their faces what they felt. Those nearest Raymond Parsloe jostled to get further away. Mrs Smethurst eyed him stonily through a raised lorgnette. One or two low hisses were heard, and over at the other end of the room somebody opened the window in a marked manner.

Raymond Parsloe Devine hesitated for a moment, then, realizing his situation, turned and slunk to the door. There was an audible sigh of relief as it closed behind him.

Vladimir Brusiloff proceeded to sum up.

'No novelists any good except me. Sovietski – yah! Nastikoff – bah! I spit me of zem all. No novelists anywhere any good except me. P. G. Wodehouse and Tolstoi not bad. Not good, but not bad. No novelists any good except me.'

And, having uttered this dictum, he removed a slab of cake from a near-by plate, steered it through the jungle, and began to champ.

It is too much to say that there was a dead silence. There could never be that in any room in which Vladimir Brusiloff was eating cake. But certainly what you might call the general chit-chat was pretty well down and out. Nobody liked to be the first to speak. The members of the Wood Hills Literary Society looked at one another timidly. Cuthbert, for his part, gazed at Adeline; and Adeline gazed into space. It was plain that the girl was deeply stirred. Her eyes were opened wide, a faint flush crimsoned her cheeks, and her breath was coming quickly.

Adeline's mind was in a whirl. She felt as if she had been walking gaily along a pleasant path and had stopped suddenly on the very brink of a precipice. It would be idle to deny that Raymond Parsloe Devine had attracted her extraordinarily. She had taken him at his own valuation as an extremely hot potato, and her hero-worship had gradually been turning into love. And now her hero had been shown to have feet of clay. It was hard, I consider, on Raymond Parsloe Devine, but that is how it goes in this world. You get a following as a celebrity, and then you run up against another bigger celebrity and your admirers desert you. One could moralize on this at considerable length, but better not, perhaps. Enough to say that the glamour of Raymond Devine ceased abruptly in that moment for Adeline, and her most coherent thought at this juncture was the resolve, as soon as she got up to her room, to burn the three signed photographs he had sent her and to give the autographed presentation set of his books to the grocer's boy.

Mrs Smethurst, meanwhile, having rallied somewhat, was endeavouring to set the feast of reason and flow of soul going again.

'And how do you like England, Mr Brusiloff?' she asked.

The celebrity paused in the act of lowering another segment of cake.

'Dam good,' he replied, cordially.

'I suppose you have travelled all over the country by this time?'

'You said it,' agreed the Thinker.

'Have you met many of our great public men?'

'Yais – Yais – Quite a few of the nibs – Lloyid Gorge, I meet him. But—' Beneath the matting a discontented expression came into his face, and his voice took on a peevish note. 'But I not meet your *real* great men – your Arbmishel, your Arreevadon – I not meet them. That's what gives me the pipovitch. Have *you* ever met Arbmishel and Arreevadon?'

A strained, anguished look came into Mrs Smethurst's face and was reflected in the faces of the other members of the circle. The eminent Russian had sprung two entirely new ones on them, and they felt that their ignorance was about to be exposed. What would Vladimir Brusiloff think of the Wood Hills Literary Society? The reputation of the Wood Hills Literary Society was at stake, trembling in the balance, and coming up for the third time. In dumb agony Mrs Smethurst rolled her eyes about the room searching for someone capable of coming to the rescue. She drew blank.

And then, from a distant corner, there sounded a deprecating cough, and those nearest Cuthbert Banks saw that he had stopped twisting his right foot round his left ankle and his left foot round his right ankle and was sitting up with a light of almost human intelligence in his eyes.

'Er—' said Cuthbert, blushing as every eye in the room seemed to fix itself on him, 'I think he means Abe Mitchell and Harry Vardon.'

'Abe Mitchell and Harry Vardon?' repeated Mrs Smethurst, blankly. 'I never heard of—'

'Yais! Yais! Most! Very!' shouted Vladimir Brusiloff, enthusiastically. 'Arbmishel and Arreevadon. You know them, yes, what, no, perhaps?'

'I've played with Abe Mitchell often, and I was partnered with Harry Vardon in last year's Open.'

The great Russian uttered a cry that shook the chandelier.

'You play in ze Open? Why,' he demanded reproachfully of Mrs Smethurst, 'was I not been introduced to this young man who play in opens?'

'Well, really,' faltered Mrs Smethurst. 'Well, the fact is, Mr Brusiloff—'

She broke off. She was unequal to the task of explaining, without hurting anyone's feelings, that she had always regarded Cuthbert as a piece of cheese and a blot on the landscape.

'Introduct me!' thundered the Celebrity.

'Why, certainly, certainly, of course. This is Mr—.' She looked appealingly at Cuthbert.

'Banks,' prompted Cuthbert.

'Banks!' cried Vladimir Brusiloff. 'Not Cootaboot Banks?'

'*Is* your name Cootaboot?' asked Mrs Smethurst, faintly.

'Well, it's Cuthbert.'

'Yais! Yais! Cootaboot!' There was a rush and swirl, as the effervescent Muscovite burst his way through the throng and rushed to where Cuthbert sat. He stood for a moment eyeing him excitedly, then, stooping swiftly, kissed him on both cheeks before Cuthbert could get his guard up. 'My dear young man, I saw you win ze French Open. Great! Great! Grand! Superb! Hot stuff, and you can say I said so! Will you permit one who is but eighteen at Nijni-Novgorod to salute you once more?'

And he kissed Cuthbert again. Then, brushing aside one or two intellectuals who were in the way, he dragged up a chair and sat down.

'You are a great man!' he said.

'Oh, no,' said Cuthbert modestly.

'Yais! Great. Most! Very! The way you lay your approach-putts dead from anywhere!'

'Oh, I don't know.'

Mr Brusiloff drew his chair closer.

'Let me tell you one vairy funny story about putting. It was one day I play at Nijni-Novgorod with the pro. against Lenin and Trotsky, and Trotsky had a two-inch putt for the hole. But, just as he addresses the ball, someone in the crowd he tries to assassinate Lenin with a rewolwer – you know that is our great national sport, trying to assassinate Lenin with rewolwers – and the bang puts Trotsky off his stroke and he goes five yards past the hole, and then Lenin, who is rather shaken, you understand, he misses again himself, and we win the hole and match and I clean up three hundred and ninety-six thousand roubles, or fifteen shillings in your money. Some gameovitch! And now let me tell you one other vairy funny story—'

Desultory conversation had begun in murmurs over the rest of the room, as the Wood Hills intellectuals politely endeavoured to conceal the fact that they realized that they were about as much out of it at this reunion of twin souls as cats at a dog-show. From time to time they started as Vladimir Brusiloff's laugh boomed out. Perhaps it was a consolation to them to know that he was enjoying himself.

As for Adeline, how shall I describe her emotions? She was stunned. Before her very eyes the stone which the builders had rejected had become the main thing, the hundred-to-one shot had walked away with the race. A rush of tender admiration for Cuthbert Banks flooded her heart. She saw that she had been all wrong. Cuthbert, whom she had always treated with a patronizing superiority, was really a man to be looked up to and worshipped. A deep, dreamy sigh shook Adeline's fragile form.

Half an hour later Vladimir and Cuthbert Banks rose.

'Goot-a-bye, Mrs Smet-thirst,' said the Celebrity. 'Zank you for a most charming visit. My friend Cootaboot and me we go now to shoot a few holes. You will lend me clobs, friend Cootaboot?'

'Any you want.'

'The niblicksky is what I use most. Goot-a-bye, Mrs Smet-thirst.'

They were moving to the door, when Cuthbert felt a light touch on his arm. Adeline was looking up at him tenderly.

'May I come, too, and walk round with you?'

Cuthbert's bosom heaved.

'Oh,' he said, with a tremor in his voice, 'that you would walk round with me for life!'

Her eyes met his.

'Perhaps,' she whispered, softly, 'it could be arranged.'

*   *   *   *   *   *   *   *   *

'And so,' (concluded the Oldest Member), 'you see that golf can be of the greatest practical assistance to a man in Life's struggle. Raymond Parsloe Devine, who was no player, had to move out of the neighbourhood immediately, and is now, I believe, writing scenarios out in California for the Flicker Film Company. Adeline is married to Cuthbert, and it was only his earnest pleading which prevented her from having their eldest son christened Abe Mitchell Ribbed-Faced Mashie Banks, for she is now as keen a devotee of the great game as her husband. Those who know them say that theirs is a union so devoted, so—'

*   *   *   *   *   *   *   *   *

The Sage broke off abruptly, for the young man had rushed to the door and out into the passage. Through the open door he could hear him crying passionately to the waiter to bring back his clubs.

2 A WOMAN IS ONLY A WOMAN

On a fine day in the spring, summer, or early autumn, there are few spots more delightful than the terrace in front of our Golf Club. It is a vantage-point peculiarly fitted to the man of philosophic mind: for from it may be seen that varied, never-ending pageant, which men call Golf, in a number of its aspects. To your right, on the first tee, stand the cheery optimists who are about to make their opening drive, happily conscious that even a topped shot will trickle a measurable distance down the steep hill. Away in the valley, directly in front of you, is the lake hole, where these same optimists will be converted to pessimism by the wet splash of a new ball. At your side is the ninth green, with its sinuous undulations which have so often wrecked the returning traveller in sight of home. And at various points within your line of vision are the third tee, the sixth tee, and the sinister bunkers about the eighth green – none of them lacking in food for the reflective mind.

It is on this terrace that the Oldest Member sits, watching the younger generation knocking at the divot. His gaze wanders from Jimmy Fothergill's two-hundred-and-twenty-yard drive down the hill to the silver drops that flash up in the sun, as young Freddie Woosley's mashie-shot drops weakly into the waters of the lake. Returning, it rests upon Peter Willard, large and tall, and James Todd, small and slender, as they struggle up the fairway of the ninth.

* * * * * * * * *

Love (says the Oldest Member) is an emotion which your true golfer should always treat with suspicion. Do not misunderstand me. I am not saying that love is a bad thing, only that it is an unknown quantity. I have known cases where marriage improved a man's game, and other cases where it seemed to put him right off his stroke. There seems to be no fixed rule. But what I do say is that a golfer should be cautious. He should not be led away by the first pretty face. I will tell you a story that illustrates the point. It is the story of those two men who have just got on to the ninth green – Peter Willard and James Todd.

There is about great friendships between man and man (said the Oldest Member) a certain inevitability that can only be compared with the age-old association of ham and eggs. No one can say when it was that these two wholesome and palatable foodstuffs first came together, nor what was the mutual magnetism that brought their deathless partnership about. One simply feels that it is one of the things that must be so. Similarly with men. Who can trace to its first beginnings the love of Damon for Pythias, of David for Jonathan, of Swan for Edgar? Who can explain what it was about Crosse that first attracted Blackwell? We simply say, 'These men are friends,' and leave it at that.

In the case of Peter Willard and James Todd, one may hazard the guess that the first link in the chain that bound them together was the fact that they took up golf within a few days of each other, and contrived, as time went on, to develop such equal form at the game that the most expert critics are still baffled in their efforts to decide which is the worse player. I have heard the point argued a hundred times without any conclusion being reached. Supporters of Peter claim that his driving off the tee entitles him to an unchallenged pre-eminence among the world's most hopeless foozlers – only to be discomfited later when the advocates of James show, by means of diagrams, that no one has ever surpassed their man in absolute incompetence with the spoon. It is one of those problems where debate is futile.

Few things draw two men together more surely than a mutual inability to master golf, coupled with an intense and ever-increasing love for the game. At the end of the first few months, when a series of costly experiments had convinced both Peter and James that there was not a tottering grey-beard nor a toddling infant in the neighbourhood whose downfall they could encompass, the two became inseparable. It was pleasanter, they found, to play together, and go neck and neck round the eighteen holes, than to take on some lissome youngster who could spatter them all over the course with one old ball and a cut-down cleek stolen from his father; or some spavined elder who not only rubbed it into them, but was apt, between strokes, to bore them with personal reminiscences of the Crimean War. So they began to play together early and late. In the small hours before breakfast, long ere the first faint piping of the waking caddie made itself heard from the caddie-shed, they were half-way through their opening round. And, at close of day, when bats wheeled against the steely sky and the 'pro's' had stolen home to rest, you might see them in the deepening dusk, going through the concluding exercises of their final spasm. After dark, they visited each other's houses and read golf books.

If you have gathered from what I have said that Peter Willard and James Todd were fond of golf, I am satisfied. That is the impression I intended to convey. They were real golfers, for real golf is a thing of the spirit, not of mere mechanical excellence of stroke.

It must not be thought, however, that they devoted too much of their time and their thoughts to golf – assuming, indeed, that such a thing is possible. Each was connected with a business in the metropolis; and often, before he left for the links, Peter would go to the trouble and expense of ringing up the office to say he would not be coming in that day; while I myself have heard James – and this not once, but frequently – say, while lunching in the club-house, that he had half a mind to get Gracechurch Street on the 'phone and ask how things were going. They were, in fact, the type of men of whom England is proudest – the backbone of a great country, toilers in the mart, untired business men, keen red-blooded men of affairs. If they played a little golf besides, who shall blame them?

So they went on, day by day, happy and contented. And then the Woman came into their lives, like the Serpent in the Links of Eden, and perhaps for the first time they realized that they were not one entity – not one single, indivisible Something that made for topped drives and short putts – but two individuals, in whose breasts Nature had implanted other desires than the simple ambition some day to do the dog-leg hole on the second nine in under double figures. My friends tell me that, when I am relating a story, my language is inclined at times a little to obscure my meaning; but, if you understand from what I have been saying that James Todd and Peter Willard both fell in love with the same woman – all right, let us carry on. That is precisely what I was driving at.

I have not the pleasure of an intimate acquaintance with Grace Forrester. I have seen her in the distance, watering the flowers in her garden, and on these occasions her stance struck me as graceful. And once, at a picnic, I observed her killing wasps with a teaspoon, and was impressed by the freedom of the wrist-action of her back-swing. Beyond this, I can say little. But she must have been attractive, for there can be no doubt of the earnestness with which both Peter and James fell in love with her. I doubt if either slept a wink the night of the dance at which it was their privilege first to meet her.

The next afternoon, happening to encounter Peter in the bunker near the eleventh green, James said: –

'That was a nice girl, that Miss What's-her-name.'

And Peter, pausing for a moment from his trench-digging, replied: –

'Yes.'

And then James, with a pang, knew that he had a rival, for he had not mentioned Miss Forrester's name, and yet Peter had divined that it was to her that he had referred.

Love is a fever which, so to speak, drives off without wasting time on the address. On the very next morning after the conversation which I have related, James Todd rang Peter Willard up on the 'phone and cancelled their golf engagements for the day, on the plea of a sprained wrist. Peter, acknowledging the cancellation, stated that he himself had been on the point of ringing James up to say that he would be unable to play owing to a slight headache. They met at tea-time at Miss Forrester's house. James asked how Peter's headache was, and Peter said it was a little better. Peter inquired after James's sprained wrist, and was told it seemed on the mend. Miss Forrester dispensed tea and conversation to both impartially.

They walked home together. After an awkward silence of twenty minutes, James said: –

'There is something about the atmosphere – the aura, shall I say? – that emanates from a good woman that makes a man feel that life has a new, a different meaning.'

Peter replied: –

'Yes.'

When they reached James's door, James said: –

'I won't ask you in to-night, old man. You want to go home and rest and cure that headache.'

'Yes,' said Peter.

There was another silence. Peter was thinking that, only a couple of days before, James had told him that he had a copy of Sandy MacBean's 'How to Become a Scratch Man Your First Season by Studying Photographs' coming by parcel-post from town, and they had arranged to read it aloud together. By now, thought Peter, it must be lying on his friend's table. The thought saddened him. And James, guessing what was in Peter's mind, was saddened too. But he did not waver. He was in no mood to read MacBean's masterpiece that night. In the twenty minutes of silence after leaving Miss Forrester he had realized that 'Grace' rhymes with 'face', and he wanted to sit alone in his study and write poetry. The two men parted with a distant nod. I beg your pardon? Yes, you are right. Two distant nods. It was always a failing of mine to count the score erroneously.

It is not my purpose to weary you by a minute recital of the happenings of each day that went by. On the surface, the lives of these two men seemed unchanged. They still played golf together, and during the round achieved towards each other a manner that, superficially, retained all its ancient cheeriness and affection. If – I should say – when, James topped his drive, Peter never failed to say 'Hard luck!' And when – or, rather, if Peter managed not to top his, James invariably said 'Great!' But things were not the same, and they knew it.

It so happened, as it sometimes will on these occasions, for Fate is a dramatist who gets his best effects with a small cast, that Peter Willard and James Todd were the only visible aspirants for the hand of Miss Forrester. Right at the beginning young Freddie Woosley had seemed attracted by the girl, and had called once or twice with flowers and chocolates, but Freddie's affections never centred themselves on one object for more than a few days, and he had dropped out after the first week. From that time on it became clear to all of us that, if Grace Forrester intended to marry anyone in the place, it would be either James or Peter; and a good deal of interest was taken in the matter by the local sportsmen. So little was known of the form of the two men, neither having figured as principal in a love-affair before, that even money was the best you could get, and the market was sluggish. I think my own flutter of twelve golf-balls, taken up by Percival Brown, was the most substantial of any of the wagers. I selected James as the winner. Why, I can hardly say, unless that he had an aunt who contributed occasional stories to the *Woman's Sphere*. These things sometimes weigh with a girl. On the other hand, George Lucas, who had half-a-dozen of ginger-ale on Peter, based his calculations on the fact that James wore knickerbockers on the links, and that no girl could possibly love a man with calves like that. In short, you see, we really had nothing to go on.

Nor had James and Peter. The girl seemed to like them both equally. They never saw her except in each other's company. And it was not until one day that Grace Forrester was knitting a sweater that there seemed a chance of getting a clue to her hidden feelings.

When the news began to spread through the place that Grace was knitting this sweater there was a big sensation. The thing seemed to us practically to amount to a declaration.

That was the view that James Todd and Peter Willard took of it, and they used to call on Grace, watch her knitting, and come away with their heads full of complicated calculations. The whole thing hung on one point – to wit, what size the sweater was going to be. If it was large, then it must be for Peter; if small, then James was the lucky man. Neither dared to make open inquiries, but it began to seem almost impossible to find out the truth without them. No masculine eye can reckon up purls and plains and estimate the size of chest which the garment is destined to cover. Moreover, with amateur knitters there must always be allowed a margin for involuntary error. There were many cases during the war where our girls sent sweaters to their sweethearts which would have induced strangulation in their young brothers. The amateur sweater of those days was, in fact, practically tantamount to German propaganda.

Peter and James were accordingly baffled. One evening the sweater would look small, and James would come away jubilant; the next it would have swollen over a vast area, and Peter would walk home singing. The suspense of the two men can readily be imagined. On the one hand, they wanted to know their fate; on the other, they fully realized that whoever the sweater was for would have to wear it. And, as it was vivid pink and would probably not fit by a mile, their hearts quailed at the prospect.

In all affairs of human tension there must come a breaking point. It came one night as the two men were walking home.

'Peter,' said James, stopping in mid-stride. He mopped his forehead. His manner had been feverish all the evening.

'Yes?' said Peter.

'I can't stand this any longer. I haven't had a good night's rest for weeks. We must find out definitely which of us is to have that sweater.'

'Let's go back and ask her,' said Peter.

So they turned back and rang the bell and went into the house and presented themselves before Miss Forrester.

'Lovely evening,' said James, to break the ice.

'Superb,' said Peter.

'Delightful,' said Miss Forrester, looking a little surprised at finding the troupe playing a return date without having booked it in advance.

'To settle a bet,' said James, 'will you please tell us who – I should say, whom – you are knitting that sweater for?'

'It is not a sweater,' replied Miss Forrester, with a womanly candour that well became her. 'It is a sock. And it is for my cousin Juliet's youngest son, Willie.'

'Good night,' said James.

'Good night,' said Peter.

'Good night,' said Grace Forrester.

It was during the long hours of the night, when ideas so often come to wakeful men, that James was struck by an admirable solution of his and Peter's difficulty. It seemed to him that, were one or the other to leave Woodhaven, the survivor would find himself in a position to conduct his wooing as wooing should be conducted. Hitherto, as I have indicated, neither had allowed the other to be more than a few minutes alone with the girl. They watched each other like hawks. When James called, Peter called. When Peter dropped in, James invariably popped round. The thing had resolved itself into a stalemate.

The idea which now came to James was that he and Peter should settle their rivalry by an eighteen-hole match on the links. He thought very highly of the idea before he finally went to sleep, and in the morning the scheme looked just as good to him as it had done overnight.

James was breakfasting next morning, preparatory to going round to disclose his plan to Peter, when Peter walked in, looking happier than he had done for days.

''Morning,' said James.

''Morning,' said Peter.

Peter sat down and toyed absently with a slice of bacon.

'I've got an idea,' he said.

'One isn't many,' said James, bringing his knife down with a jerk-shot on a fried egg. 'What is your idea?'

'Got it last night as I was lying awake. It struck me that, if either of us was to clear out of this place, the other would have a fair chance. You know what I mean – with Her. At present we've got each other stymied. Now, how would it be,' said Peter, abstractedly spreading marmalade on his bacon, 'if we were to play an eighteen-hole match, the loser to leg out of the neighbourhood and stay away long enough to give the winner the chance to find out exactly how things stood?'

James started so violently that he struck himself in the left eye with his fork.

'That's exactly the idea I got last night, too.'

'Then it's a go?'

'It's the only thing to do.'

There was silence for a moment. Both men were thinking. Remember, they were friends. For years they had shared each other's sorrows, joys, and golf-balls, and sliced into the same bunkers.

Presently Peter said: –

'I shall miss you.'

'What do you mean, miss me?'

'When you're gone. Woodhaven won't seem the same place. But of course you'll soon be able to come back. I sha'n't waste any time proposing.'

'Leave me your address,' said James, 'and I'll send you a wire when you can return. You won't be offended if I don't ask you to be best man at the wedding? In the circumstances it might be painful to you.'

Peter sighed dreamily.

'We'll have the sitting-room done in blue. Her eyes are blue.'

'Remember,' said James, 'there will always be a knife and fork for you at our little nest. Grace is not the woman to want me to drop my bachelor friends.'

'Touching this match,' said Peter. 'Strict Royal and Ancient rules, of course?'

'Certainly.'

'I mean to say – no offence, old man – but no grounding niblicks in bunkers.'

'Precisely. And, without hinting at anything personal, the ball shall be considered holed-out only when it is in the hole, not when it stops on the edge.'

'Undoubtedly. And – you know I don't want to hurt your feelings – missing the ball counts as a stroke, not as a practice-swing.'

'Exactly. And – you'll forgive me if I mention it – a player whose ball has fallen in the rough, may not pull up all the bushes within a radius of three feet.'

'In fact, strict rules.'

'Strict rules.'

They shook hands without more words. And presently Peter walked out, and James, with a guilty look over his shoulder, took down Sandy MacBean's great work from the bookshelf and began to study the photograph of the short approach-shot showing Mr MacBean swinging from Point A, through dotted line B–C, to Point D, his head the while remaining rigid at the spot marked with a cross. He felt a little guiltily that he had stolen a march on his friend, and that the contest was as good as over.

* * * * * * * * *

I cannot recall a lovelier summer day than that on which the great Todd–Willard eighteen-hole match took place. It had rained during the night, and now the sun shone down from a clear blue sky on to turf that glistened more greenly than the young grass of early spring. Butterflies flitted to and fro; birds sang merrily. In short, all Nature smiled. And it is to be doubted if Nature ever had a better excuse for smiling – or even laughing outright; for matches like that between James Todd and Peter Willard do not occur every day.

Whether it was that love had keyed them up, or whether hours of study of Braid's 'Advanced Golf' and the Badminton Book had produced a belated effect, I cannot say; but both started off quite reasonably well. Our first hole, as you can see, is a bogey four, and James was dead on the pin in seven, leaving Peter, who had twice hit the United Kingdom with his mashie in mistake for the ball, a difficult putt for the half. Only one thing could happen when you left Peter a difficult putt; and James advanced to the lake-hole one up, Peter, as he followed, trying to console himself with the thought that many of the best golfers prefer to lose the first hole and save themselves for a strong finish.

Peter and James had played over the lake-hole so often that they had become accustomed to it, and had grown into the habit of sinking a ball or two as a preliminary formality with much the same stoicism displayed by those kings in ancient and superstitious times who used to fling jewellery into the sea to propitiate it before they took a voyage. But to-day, by one of those miracles without which golf would not be golf, each of them got over with his first shot – and not only over, but dead on the pin. Our 'pro.' himself could not have done better.

I think it was at this point that the two men began to go to pieces. They were in an excited frame of mind, and this thing unmanned them. You will no doubt recall Keats's poem about stout Cortes staring with eagle eyes at the Pacific while all his men gazed at each other with a wild surmise, silent upon a peak in Darien. Precisely so did Peter Willard and James Todd stare with eagle eyes at the second lake-hole, and gaze at each other with a wild surmise, silent upon a tee in Woodhaven. They had dreamed of such a happening so often and woke to find the vision false, that at first they could not believe that the thing had actually occurred.

'I got over!' whispered James, in an awed voice.

'So did I!' muttered Peter.

'In one!'

'With my very first!'

They walked in silence round the edge of the lake, and holed out. One putt was enough for each, and they halved the hole with a two. Peter's previous record was eight, and James had once done a seven. There are times when strong men lose their self-control, and this was one of them. They reached the third tee in a daze, and it was here that mortification began to set in.

The third hole is another bogey four, up the hill and past the tree that serves as a direction-post, the hole itself being out of sight. On his day, James had often done it in ten and Peter in nine; but now they were unnerved. James, who had the honour, shook visibly as he addressed his ball. Three times he swung and only connected with the ozone; the fourth time he topped badly. The discs had been set back a little way, and James had the mournful distinction of breaking a record for the course by playing his fifth shot from the tee. It was a low, raking brassey-shot, which carried a heap of stones twenty feet to the right and finished in a furrow. Peter, meanwhile, had popped up a lofty ball which came to rest behind a stone.

It was now that the rigid rules governing this contest began to take their toll. Had they been playing an ordinary friendly round, each would have teed up on some convenient hillock and probably been past the tree with their second, for James would, in ordinary circumstances, have taken his drive back and regarded the strokes he had made as a little preliminary practice to get him into mid-season form. But to-day it was war to the niblick, and neither man asked nor expected quarter. Peter's seventh shot dislodged the stone, leaving him a clear field, and James, with his eleventh, extricated himself from the furrow. Fifty feet from the tree James was eighteen, Peter twelve; but then the latter, as every golfer does at times, suddenly went right off his game. He hit the tree four times, then hooked into the sand-bunkers to the left of the hole. James, who had been playing a game that was steady without being brilliant, was on the green in twenty-six, Peter taking twenty-seven. Poor putting lost James the hole. Peter was down in thirty-three, but the pace was too hot for James. He missed a two-foot putt for the half, and they went to the fourth tee all square.

The fourth hole follows the curve of the road, on the other side of which are picturesque woods. It presents no difficulties to the expert, but it has pitfalls for the novice. The dashing player stands for a slice, while the more cautious are satisfied if they can clear the bunker that spans the fairway and lay their ball well out to the left, whence an iron shot will take them to the green. Peter and James combined the two policies. Peter aimed to the left and got a slice, and James, also aiming to the left, topped into the bunker. Peter, realizing from experience the futility of searching for his ball in the woods, drove a second, which also disappeared into the jungle, as did his third. By the time he had joined James in the bunker he had played his sixth.

It is the glorious uncertainty of golf that makes it the game it is. The fact that James and Peter, lying side by side in the same bunker, had played respectively one and six shots, might have induced an unthinking observer to fancy the chances of the former. And no doubt, had he not taken seven strokes to extricate himself from the pit, while his opponent, by some act of God, contrived to get out in two, James's chances might have been extremely rosy. As it was, the two men staggered out on to the fairway again with a score of eight apiece. Once past the bunker and round the bend of the road, the hole becomes simple. A judicious use of the cleek put Peter on the green in fourteen, while James, with a Braid iron, reached it in twelve. Peter was down in seventeen, and James contrived to halve. It was only as he was leaving the hole that the latter discovered that he had been putting with his niblick, which cannot have failed to exercise a prejudicial effect on his game. These little incidents are bound to happen when one is in a nervous and highly-strung condition.

The fifth and sixth holes produced no unusual features. Peter won the fifth in eleven, and James the sixth in ten. The short seventh they halved in nine. The eighth, always a tricky hole, they took no liberties with, James, sinking a long putt with his twenty-third, just managing to halve. A ding-dong race up the hill for the ninth found James first at the pin, and they finished the first nine with James one up.

As they left the green James looked a little furtively at his companion.

'You might be strolling on to the tenth,' he said. 'I want to get a few balls at the shop. And my mashie wants fixing up. I sha'n't be long.'

'I'll come with you,' said Peter.

'Don't bother,' said James. 'You go on and hold our place at the tee.'

I regret to say that James was lying. His mashie was in excellent repair, and he still had a dozen balls in his bag, it being his prudent practice always to start out with eighteen. No! What he had said was mere subterfuge. He wanted to go to his locker and snatch a few minutes with Sandy MacBean's 'How to Become a Scratch Man'. He felt sure that one more glance at the photograph of Mr MacBean driving would give him the mastery of the stroke and so enable him to win the match. In this I think he was a little sanguine. The difficulty about Sandy MacBean's method of tuition was that he laid great stress on the fact that the ball should be directly in a line with a point exactly in the centre of the back of the player's neck; and so far James's efforts to keep his eye on the ball and on the back of his neck simultaneously had produced no satisfactory results.

* * * * * * * * *

It seemed to James, when he joined Peter on the tenth tee, that the latter's manner was strange. He was pale. There was a curious look in his eye.

'James, old man,' he said.

'Yes?' said James.

'While you were away I have been thinking. James, old man, do you really love this girl?'

James stared. A spasm of pain twisted Peter's face.

'Suppose,' he said in a low voice, 'she were not all you – we – think she is!'

'What do you mean?'

'Nothing, nothing.'

'Miss Forrester is an angel.'

'Yes, yes. Quite so.'

'I know what it is,' said James, passionately. 'You're trying to put me off my stroke. You know that the least thing makes me lose my form.'

'No, no!'

'You hope that you can take my mind off the game and make me go to pieces, and then you'll win the match.'

'On the contrary,' said Peter, 'I intend to forfeit the match.'

James reeled.

'What!'

'I give up.'

'But – but—' James shook with emotion. His voice quavered. 'Ah!' he cried. 'I see now: I understand! You are doing this for me because I am your pal. Peter, this is noble! This is the sort of thing you read about in books. I've seen it in the movies. But I can't accept the sacrifice.'

'You must!'

'No, no!'

'I insist!'

'Do you mean this?'

'I give her up, James, old man. I – I hope you will be happy.'

'But I don't know what to say. How can I thank you?'

'Don't thank me.'

'But, Peter, do you fully realize what you are doing? True, I am one up, but there are nine holes to go, and I am not right on my game to-day. You might easily beat me. Have you forgotten that I once took forty-seven at the dog-leg hole? This may be one of my bad days. Do you understand that if you insist on giving up I shall go to Miss Forrester to-night and propose to her?'

'I understand.'

'And yet you stick to it that you are through?'

'I do. And, by the way, there's no need for you to wait till to-night. I saw Miss Forrester just now outside the tennis court. She's alone.'

James turned crimson.

'Then I think perhaps—'

'You'd better go to her at once.'

'I will.' James extended his hand. 'Peter, old man, I shall never forget this.'

'That's all right.'

'What are you going to do?'

'Now, do you mean? Oh, I shall potter round the second nine. If you want me, you'll find me somewhere about.'

'You'll come to the wedding, Peter?' said James, wistfully.

'Of course,' said Peter. 'Good luck.'

He spoke cheerily, but, when the other had turned to go, he stood looking after him thoughtfully. Then he sighed a heavy sigh.

* * * * * * * * *

James approached Miss Forrester with a beating heart. She made a charming picture as she stood there in the sunlight, one hand on her hip, the other swaying a tennis racket.

'How do you do?' said James.

'How are you, Mr Todd? Have you been playing golf?'

'Yes.'

'With Mr Willard?'

'Yes. We were having a match.'

'Golf,' said Grace Forrester, 'seems to make men very rude. Mr Willard left me without a word in the middle of our conversation.'

James was astonished.

'Were you talking to Peter?'

'Yes. Just now. I can't understand what was the matter with him. He just turned on his heel and swung off.'

'You oughtn't to turn on your heel when you swing,' said James; 'only on the ball of the foot.'

'I beg your pardon?'

'Nothing, nothing. I wasn't thinking. The fact is, I've something on my mind. So has Peter. You mustn't think too hardly of him. We have been playing an important match, and it must have got on his nerves. You didn't happen by any chance to be watching us?'

'No.'

'Ah! I wish you had seen me at the lake-hole. I did it one under par.'

'Was your father playing?'

'You don't understand. I mean I did it in one better than even the finest player is supposed to do it. It's a mashie-shot, you know. You mustn't play too light, or you fall in the lake; and you mustn't play it too hard, or you go past the hole into the woods. It requires the nicest delicacy and judgement, such as I gave it. You might have to wait a year before seeing anyone do it in two again. I doubt if the "pro." often does it in two. Now, directly we came to this hole to-day, I made up my mind that there was going to be no mistake. The great secret of any shot at golf is ease, elegance, and the ability to relax. The majority of men, you will find, think it important that their address should be good.'

'How snobbish! What does it matter where a man lives?'

'You don't absolutely follow me. I refer to the waggle and the stance before you make the stroke. Most players seem to fix in their minds the appearance of the angles which are presented by the position of the arms, legs, and club shaft, and it is largely the desire to retain these angles which results in their moving their heads and stiffening their muscles so that there is no freedom in the swing. There is only one point which vitally affects the stroke, and the only reason why that should be kept constant is that you are enabled to see your ball clearly. That is the pivotal point marked at the base of the neck, and a line drawn from this point to the ball should be at right angles to the line of flight.'

James paused for a moment for air, and as he paused Miss Forrester spoke.

'This is all gibberish to me,' she said.

'Gibberish!' gasped James. 'I am quoting verbatim from one of the best authorities on golf.'

Miss Forrester swung her tennis racket irritably.

'Golf,' she said, 'bores me pallid. I think it is the silliest game ever invented!'

The trouble about telling a story is that words are so feeble a means of depicting the supreme moments of life. That is where the artist has the advantage over the historian. Were I an artist, I should show James at this point falling backwards with his feet together and his eyes shut, with a semi-circular dotted line marking the progress of his flight and a few stars above his head to indicate moral collapse. There are no words that can adequately describe the sheer, black horror that froze the blood in his veins as this frightful speech smote his ears.

He had never inquired into Miss Forrester's religious views before, but he had always assumed that they were sound. And now here she was polluting the golden summer air with the most hideous blasphemy. It would be incorrect to say that James's love was turned to hate. He did not hate Grace. The repulsion he felt was deeper than mere hate. What he felt was not altogether loathing and not wholly pity. It was a blend of the two.

There was a tense silence. The listening world stood still. Then, without a word, James Todd turned and tottered away.

* * * * * * * * *

Peter was working moodily in the twelfth bunker when his friend arrived. He looked up with a start. Then, seeing that the other was alone, he came forward hesitatingly.

'Am I to congratulate you?'

James breathed a deep breath.

'You are!' he said. 'On an escape!'

'She refused you?'

'She didn't get the chance. Old man, have you ever sent one right up the edge of that bunker in front of the seventh and just not gone in?'

'Very rarely.'

'I did once. It was my second shot, from a good lie, with the light iron, and I followed well through and thought I had gone just too far, and, when I walked up, there was my ball on the edge of the bunker, nicely teed up on a chunk of grass, so that I was able to lay it dead with my mashie-niblick, holing out in six. Well, what I mean to say is, I feel now as I felt then – as if some unseen power had withheld me in time from some frightful disaster.'

'I know just how you feel,' said Peter, gravely.

'Peter, old man, that girl said golf bored her pallid. She said she thought it was the silliest game ever invented.' He paused to mark the effect of his words. Peter merely smiled a faint, wan smile.

'You don't seem revolted,' said James.

'I am revolted, but not surprised. You see, she said the same thing to me only a few minutes before.'

'She did!'

'It amounted to the same thing. I had just been telling her how I did the lake-hole to-day in two, and she said that in her opinion golf was a game for children with water on the brain who weren't athletic enough to play Animal Grab.'

The two men shivered in sympathy.

'There must be insanity in the family,' said James at last.

'That,' said Peter, 'is the charitable explanation.'

'We were fortunate to find it out in time.'

'We were!'

'We mustn't run a risk like that again.'

'Never again!'

'I think we had better take up golf really seriously. It will keep us out of mischief.'

'You're quite right. We ought to do our four rounds a day regularly.'

'In spring, summer, and autumn. And in winter it would be rash not to practise most of the day at one of those indoor schools.'

'We ought to be safe that way.'

'Peter, old man,' said James, 'I've been meaning to speak to you about it for some time. I've got Sandy MacBean's new book, and I think you ought to read it. It is full of helpful hints.'

'James!'

'Peter!'

Silently the two men clasped hands. James Todd and Peter Willard were themselves again.

* * * * * * * * *

And so (said the Oldest Member) we come back to our original starting-point – to wit, that, while there is nothing to be said definitely against love, your golfer should be extremely careful how he indulges in it. It may improve his game or it may not. But, if he finds that there is any danger that it may not – if the object of his affections is not the kind of girl who will listen to him with cheerful sympathy through the long evenings, while he tells her, illustrating stance and grip and swing with the kitchen poker, each detail of the day's round – then, I say unhesitatingly, he had better leave it alone. Love has had a lot of press-agenting from the oldest times; but there are higher, nobler things than love. A woman is only a woman, but a hefty drive is a slosh.

3 A MIXED THREESOME

It was the holiday season, and during the holidays the Greens Committees have decided that the payment of twenty guineas shall entitle fathers of families not only to infest the course themselves, but also to decant their nearest and dearest upon it in whatever quantity they please. All over the links, in consequence, happy, laughing groups of children had broken out like a rash. A wan-faced adult, who had been held up for ten minutes while a drove of issue quarrelled over whether little Claude had taken two hundred or two hundred and twenty approach shots to reach the ninth green sank into a seat beside the Oldest Member.

'What luck?' inquired the Sage.

'None to speak of,' returned the other, moodily.

'I thought I had bagged a small boy in a Lord Fauntleroy suit on the sixth, but he ducked. These children make me tired. They should be bowling their hoops in the road. Golf is a game for grown-ups. How can a fellow play, with a platoon of progeny blocking him at every hole?'

The Oldest Member shook his head. He could not subscribe to these sentiments.

No doubt (said the Oldest Member) the summer golf-child is, from the point of view of the player who likes to get round the course in a single afternoon, something of a trial; but, personally, I confess, it pleases me to see my fellow human beings – and into this category golf-children, though at the moment you may not be broad-minded enough to admit it, undoubtedly fall – taking to the noblest of games at an early age. Golf, like measles, should be caught young, for, if postponed to riper years, the results may be serious. Let me tell you the story of Mortimer Sturgis, which illustrates what I mean rather aptly.

Mortimer Sturgis, when I first knew him, was a care-free man of thirty-eight, of amiable character and independent means, which he increased from time to time by judicious ventures on the Stock Exchange. Although he had never played golf, his had not been altogether an ill-spent life. He swung a creditable racket at tennis, was always ready to contribute a baritone solo to charity concerts, and gave freely to the poor. He was what you might call a golden-mean man, good-hearted rather than magnetic, with no serious vices and no heroic virtues. For a hobby, he had taken up the collecting of porcelain vases, and he was engaged to Betty Weston, a charming girl of twenty-five, a lifelong friend of mine.

I liked Mortimer. Everybody liked him. But, at the same time, I was a little surprised that a girl like Betty should have become engaged to him. As I said before, he was not magnetic; and magnetism, I thought, was the chief quality she would have demanded in a man. Betty was one of those ardent, vivid girls, with an intense capacity for hero-worship, and I would have supposed that something more in the nature of a plumed knight or a corsair of the deep would have been her ideal. But, of course, if there is a branch of modern industry where the demand is greater than the supply, it is the manufacture of knights and corsairs; and nowadays a girl, however flaming her aspirations, has to take the best she can get. I must admit that Betty seemed perfectly content with Mortimer.

Such, then, was the state of affairs when Eddie Denton arrived, and the trouble began.

I was escorting Betty home one evening after a tea-party at which we had been fellow-guests, when, walking down the road, we happened to espy Mortimer. He broke into a run when he saw us, and galloped up, waving a piece of paper in his hand. He was plainly excited, a thing which was unusual in this well-balanced man. His broad, good-humoured face was working violently.

'Good news!' he cried. 'Good news! Dear old Eddie's back!'

'Oh, how nice for you, dear!' said Betty. 'Eddie Denton is Mortimer's best friend,' she explained to me. 'He has told me so much about him. I have been looking forward to his coming home. Mortie thinks the world of him.'

'So will you, when you know him,' cried Mortimer. 'Dear old Eddie! He's a wonder! The best fellow on earth! We were at school and the 'Varsity together. There's nobody like Eddie! He landed yesterday. Just home from Central Africa. He's an explorer, you know,' he said to me. 'Spends all his time in places where it's death for a white man to go.'

'An explorer!' I heard Betty breathe, as if to herself. I was not so impressed, I fear, as she was. Explorers, as a matter of fact, leave me a trifle cold. It has always seemed to me that the difficulties of their life are greatly exaggerated – generally by themselves. In a large country like Africa, for instance, I should imagine that it was almost impossible for a man not to get somewhere if he goes on long enough. Give *me* the fellow who can plunge into the bowels of the earth at Piccadilly Circus and find the right Tube train with nothing but a lot of misleading signs to guide him. However, we are not all constituted alike in this world, and it was apparent from the flush on her cheek and the light in her eyes that Betty admired explorers.

'I wired to him at once,' went on Mortimer, 'and insisted on his coming down here. It's two years since I saw him. You don't know how I have looked forward, dear, to you and Eddie meeting. He is just your sort. I know how romantic you are and keen on adventure and all that. Well, you should hear Eddie tell the story of how he brought down the bull *bongo* with his last cartridge after all the *pongos*, or native bearers, had fled into the *dongo*, or undergrowth.'

'I should love to!' whispered Betty, her eyes glowing. I suppose to an impressionable girl these things really are of absorbing interest. For myself, *bongos* intrigue me even less than *pongos*, while *dongos* frankly bore me. 'When do you expect him?'

'He will get my wire to-night. I'm hoping we shall see the dear old fellow to-morrow afternoon some time. How surprised old Eddie will be to hear that I'm engaged. He's such a confirmed bachelor himself. He told me once that he considered the wisest thing ever said by human tongue was the Swahili proverb – "Whoso taketh a woman into his kraal depositeth himself straightway in the *wongo*." *Wongo*, he tells me, is a sort of broth composed of herbs and meat-bones, corresponding to our soup. You must get Eddie to give it you in the original Swahili. It sounds even better.'

I saw the girl's eyes flash, and there came into her face that peculiar set expression which married men know. It passed in an instant, but not before it had given me material for thought which lasted me all the way to my house and into the silent watches of the night. I was fond of Mortimer Sturgis, and I could see trouble ahead for him as plainly as though I had been a palmist reading his hand at two guineas a visit. There are other proverbs fully as wise as the one which Mortimer had translated from the Swahili, and one of the wisest is that quaint old East London saying, handed down from one generation of costermongers to another, and whispered at midnight in the wigwams of the whelk-sellers: 'Never introduce your donah to a pal.' In those seven words is contained the wisdom of the ages.

I could read the future so plainly. What but one thing could happen after Mortimer had influenced Betty's imagination with his stories of his friend's romantic career, and added the finishing touch by advertising him as a woman-hater? He might just as well have asked for his ring back at once. My heart bled for Mortimer.

I happened to call at his house on the second evening of the explorer's visit, and already the mischief had been done.

Denton was one of those lean, hard-bitten men with smouldering eyes and a brick-red complexion. He looked what he was, the man of action and enterprise. He had the wiry frame and strong jaw without which no explorer is complete, and Mortimer, beside him, seemed but a poor, soft product of our hothouse civilization. Mortimer, I forgot to say, wore glasses; and, if there is one time more than another when a man should not wear glasses, it is while a strong-faced, keen-eyed wanderer in the wilds is telling a beautiful girl the story of his adventures.

For this was what Denton was doing. My arrival seemed to have interrupted him in the middle of a narrative. He shook my hand in a strong, silent sort of way, and resumed: –

'Well, the natives seemed fairly friendly, so I decided to stay the night.'

I made a mental note never to seem fairly friendly to an explorer. If you do, he always decides to stay the night.

'In the morning they took me down to the river. At this point it widens into a *kongo*, or pool, and it was here, they told me, that the crocodile mostly lived, subsisting on the native oxen – the short-horned *jongos* – which, swept away by the current while crossing the ford above, were carried down on the *longos*, or rapids. It was not, however, till the second evening that I managed to catch sight of his ugly snout above the surface. I waited around, and on the third day I saw him suddenly come out of the water and heave his whole length on to a sandbank in mid-stream and go to sleep in the sun. He was certainly a monster – fully thirty – you have never been in Central Africa, have you, Miss Weston? No? You ought to go there! – fully fifty feet from tip to tail. There he lay, glistening. I shall never forget the sight.'

He broke off to light a cigarette. I heard Betty draw in her breath sharply. Mortimer was beaming through his glasses with the air of the owner of a dog which is astonishing a drawing-room with its clever tricks.

'And what did you do then, Mr Denton?' asked Betty, breathlessly.

'Yes, what did you do then, old chap?' said Mortimer.

Denton blew out the match and dropped it on the ash-tray.

'Eh? Oh,' he said, carelessly, 'I swam across and shot him.'

'Swam across and shot him!'

'Yes. It seemed to me that the chance was too good to be missed. Of course, I might have had a pot at him from the bank, but the chances were I wouldn't have hit him in a vital place. So I swam across to the sandbank, put the muzzle of my gun in his mouth, and pulled the trigger. I have rarely seen a crocodile so taken aback.'

'But how dreadfully dangerous!'

'Oh, danger!' Eddie Denton laughed lightly.

'One drops into the habit of taking a few risks out there, you know. Talking of *danger*, the time when things really did look a little nasty was when the wounded *gongo* cornered me in a narrow *tongo* and I only had a pocket-knife with everything in it broken except the corkscrew and the thing for taking stones out of horses' hoofs. It was like this—'

I could bear no more. I am a tender-hearted man, and I made some excuse and got away. From the expression on the girl's face I could see that it was only a question of days before she gave her heart to this romantic newcomer.

As a matter of fact, it was on the following afternoon that she called on me and told me that the worst had happened. I had known her from a child, you understand, and she always confided her troubles to me.

'I want your advice,' she began. 'I'm so wretched!'

She burst into tears. I could see the poor girl was in a highly nervous condition, so I did my best to calm her by describing how I had once done the long hole in four. My friends tell me that there is no finer soporific, and it seemed as though they may be right, for presently, just as I had reached the point where I laid my approach-putt dead from a distance of fifteen feet, she became quieter. She dried her eyes, yawned once or twice, and looked at me bravely.

'I love Eddie Denton!' she said.

'I feared as much. When did you feel this coming on?'

'It crashed on me like a thunderbolt last night after dinner. We were walking in the garden, and he was just telling me how he had been bitten by a poisonous *zongo*, when I seemed to go all giddy. When I came to myself I was in Eddie's arms. His face was pressed against mine, and he was gargling.'

'Gargling?'

'I thought so at first. But he reassured me. He was merely speaking in one of the lesser-known dialects of the Walla-Walla natives of Eastern Uganda, into which he always drops in moments of great emotion. He soon recovered sufficiently to give me a rough translation, and then I knew that he loved me. He kissed me. I kissed him. We kissed each other.'

'And where was Mortimer all this while?'

'Indoors, cataloguing his collection of vases.'

For a moment, I confess, I was inclined to abandon Mortimer's cause. A man, I felt, who could stay indoors cataloguing vases while his *fiancée* wandered in the moonlight with explorers deserved all that was coming to him. I overcame the feeling.

'Have you told him?'

'Of course not.'

'You don't think it might be of interest to him?'

'How can I tell him? It would break his heart. I am awfully fond of Mortimer. So is Eddie. We would both die rather than do anything to hurt him. Eddie is the soul of honour. He agrees with me that Mortimer must never know.'

'Then you aren't going to break off your engagement?'

'I couldn't. Eddie feels the same. He says that, unless something can be done, he will say good-bye to me and creep far, far away to some distant desert, and there, in the great stillness, broken only by the cry of the prowling *yongo*, try to forget.'

'When you say "unless something can be done", what do you mean? What can be done?'

'I thought you might have something to suggest. Don't you think it possible that somehow Mortimer might take it into his head to break the engagement himself?'

'Absurd! He loves you devotedly.'

'I'm afraid so. Only the other day I dropped one of his best vases, and he just smiled and said it didn't matter.'

'I can give you even better proof than that. This morning Mortimer came to me and asked me to give him secret lessons in golf.'

'Golf! But he despises golf.'

'Exactly. But he is going to learn it for your sake.'

'But why secret lessons?'

'Because he wants to keep it a surprise for your birthday. Now can you doubt his love?'

'I am not worthy of him!' she whispered.

The words gave me an idea.

'Suppose,' I said, 'we could convince Mortimer of that!'

'I don't understand.'

'Suppose, for instance, he could be made to believe that you were, let us say, a dipsomaniac.'

She shook her head. 'He knows that already.'

'What!'

'Yes; I told him I sometimes walked in my sleep.'

'I mean a secret drinker.'

'Nothing will induce me to pretend to be a secret drinker.'

'Then a drug-fiend?' I suggested, hopefully.

'I hate medicine.'

'I have it!' I said. 'A kleptomaniac.'

'What is that?'

'A person who steals things.'

'Oh, that's horrid.'

'Not at all. It's a perfectly ladylike thing to do. You don't know you do it.'

'But, if I don't know I do it, how do I know I do it?'

'I beg your pardon?'

'I mean, how can I tell Mortimer I do it if I don't know?'

'You don't tell him. I will tell him. I will inform him to-morrow that you called on me this afternoon and stole my watch and' – I glanced about the room – 'my silver matchbox.'

'I'd rather have that little vinaigrette.'

'You don't get either. I merely say you stole it. What will happen?'

'Mortimer will hit you with a cleek.'

'Not at all. I am an old man. My white hairs protect me. What he will do is to insist on confronting me with you and asking you to deny the foul charge.'

'And then?'

'Then you admit it and release him from his engagement.'

She sat for a while in silence. I could see that my words had made an impression.

'I think it's a splendid idea. Thank you very much.' She rose and moved to the door. 'I knew you would suggest something wonderful.' She hesitated. 'You don't think it would make it sound more plausible if I really took the vinaigrette?' she added, a little wistfully.

'It would spoil everything,' I replied, firmly, as I reached for the vinaigrette and locked it carefully in my desk.

She was silent for a moment, and her glance fell on the carpet. That, however, did not worry me. It was nailed down.

'Well, good-bye,' she said.

'*Au revoir*,' I replied. 'I am meeting Mortimer at six-thirty to-morrow. You may expect us round at your house at about eight.'

* * * * * * * * *

Mortimer was punctual at the tryst next morning. When I reached the tenth tee he was already there. We exchanged a brief greeting and I handed him a driver, outlined the essentials of grip and swing, and bade him go to it.

'It seems a simple game,' he said, as he took his stance. 'You're sure it's fair to have the ball sitting up on top of a young sand-hill like this?'

'Perfectly fair.'

'I mean, I don't want to be coddled because I'm a beginner.'

'The ball is always teed up for the drive,' I assured him.

'Oh, well, if you say so. But it seems to me to take all the element of sport out of the game. Where do I hit it?'

'Oh, straight ahead.'

'But isn't it dangerous? I mean, suppose I smash a window in that house over there?'

He indicated a charming bijou residence some five hundred yards down the fairway.

'In that case,' I replied, 'the owner comes out in his pyjamas and offers you the choice between some nuts and a cigar.'

He seemed reassured, and began to address the ball. Then he paused again.

'Isn't there something you say before you start?' he asked. '"Five," or something?'

'You may say "Fore!" if it makes you feel any easier. But it isn't necessary.'

'If I am going to learn this silly game,' said Mortimer, firmly, 'I am going to learn it *right*. Fore!'

I watched him curiously. I never put a club into the hand of a beginner without something of the feeling of the sculptor who surveys a mass of shapeless clay. I experience the emotions of a creator. Here, I say to myself, is a semi-sentient being into whose soulless carcass I am breathing life. A moment before, he was, though technically living, a mere clod. A moment hence he will be a golfer.

While I was still occupied with these meditations Mortimer swung at the ball. The club, whizzing down, brushed the surface of the rubber sphere, toppling it off the tee and propelling it six inches with a slight slice on it.

'Damnation!' said Mortimer, unravelling himself.

I nodded approvingly. His drive had not been anything to write to the golfing journals about, but he was picking up the technique of the game.

'What happened then?'

I told him in a word.

'Your stance was wrong, and your grip was wrong, and you moved your head, and swayed your body, and took your eye off the ball, and pressed, and forgot to use your wrists, and swung back too fast, and let the hands get ahead of the club, and lost your balance, and omitted to pivot on the ball of the left foot, and bent your right knee.'

He was silent for a moment.

'There is more in this pastime,' he said, 'than the casual observer would suspect.'

I have noticed, and I suppose other people have noticed, that in the golf education of every man there is a definite point at which he may be said to have crossed the dividing line – the Rubicon, as it were – that separates the golfer from the non-golfer. This moment comes immediately after his first good drive. In the ninety minutes in which I instructed Mortimer Sturgis that morning in the rudiments of the game, he made every variety of drive known to science; but it was not till we were about to leave that he made a good one.

A moment before he had surveyed his blistered hands with sombre disgust.

'It's no good,' he said. 'I shall never learn this beast of a game. And I don't want to either. It's only fit for lunatics. Where's the sense in it? Hitting a rotten little ball with a stick! If I want exercise, I'll take a stick and go and rattle it along the railings. There's something *in* that! Well, let's be getting along. No good wasting the whole morning out here.'

'Try one more drive, and then we'll go.'

'All right. If you like. No sense in it, though.'

He teed up the ball, took a careless stance, and flicked moodily. There was a sharp crack, the ball shot off the tee, flew a hundred yards in a dead straight line never ten feet above the ground, soared another seventy yards in a graceful arc, struck the turf, rolled, and came to rest within easy mashie distance of the green.

'Splendid!' I cried.

The man seemed stunned.

'How did that happen?'

I told him very simply.

'Your stance was right, and your grip was right, and you kept your head still, and didn't sway your body, and never took your eye off the ball, and slowed back, and let the arms come well through, and rolled the wrists, and let the club-head lead, and kept your balance, and pivoted on the ball of the left foot, and didn't duck the right knee.'

'I see,' he said. 'Yes, I thought that must be it.'

'Now let's go home.'

'Wait a minute. I just want to remember what I did while it's fresh in my mind. Let me see, this was the way I stood. Or was it more like this? No, like this.' He turned to me, beaming. 'What a great idea it was, my taking up golf! It's all nonsense what you read in the comic papers about people foozling all over the place and breaking clubs and all that. You've only to exercise a little reasonable care. And what a corking game it is! Nothing like it in the world! I wonder if Betty is up yet. I must go round and show her how I did that drive. A perfect swing, with every ounce of weight, wrist, and muscle behind it. I meant to keep it a secret from the dear girl till I had really learned, but of course I *have* learned now. Let's go round and rout her out.'

He had given me my cue. I put my hand on his shoulder and spoke sorrowfully.

'Mortimer, my boy, I fear I have bad news for you.'

'Slow back – keep the head— What's that? Bad news?'

'About Betty.'

'About Betty? What about her? Don't sway the body – keep the eye on the—'

'Prepare yourself for a shock, my boy. Yesterday afternoon Betty called to see me. When she had gone I found that she had stolen my silver matchbox.'

'Stolen your matchbox?'

'Stolen my matchbox.'

'Oh, well, I dare say there were faults on both sides,' said Mortimer. 'Tell me if I sway my body this time.'

'You don't grasp what I have said! Do you realize that Betty, the girl you are going to marry, is a kleptomaniac?'

'A kleptomaniac!'

'That is the only possible explanation. Think what this means, my boy. Think how you will feel every time your wife says she is going out to do a little shopping! Think of yourself, left alone at home, watching the clock, saying to yourself, "Now she is lifting a pair of silk stockings!" "Now she is hiding gloves in her umbrella!" "Just about this moment she is getting away with a pearl necklace!"'

'Would she do that?'

'She would! She could not help herself. Or, rather, she could not refrain from helping herself. How about it, my boy?'

'It only draws us closer together,' he said.

I was touched, I own. My scheme had failed, but it had proved Mortimer Sturgis to be of pure gold. He stood gazing down the fairway, wrapped in thought.

'By the way,' he said, meditatively, 'I wonder if the dear girl ever goes to any of those sales – those auction-sales, you know, where you're allowed to inspect the things the day before? They often have some pretty decent vases.'

He broke off and fell into a reverie.

*　　*　　*　　*　　*　　*　　*　　*　　*

From this point onward Mortimer Sturgis proved the truth of what I said to you about the perils of taking up golf at an advanced age. A lifetime of observing my fellow-creatures has convinced me that Nature intended us all to be golfers. In every human being the germ of golf is implanted at birth, and suppression causes it to grow and grow till – it may be at forty, fifty, sixty – it suddenly bursts its bonds and sweeps over the victim like a tidal wave. The wise man, who begins to play in childhood, is enabled to let the poison exude gradually from his system, with no harmful results. But a man like Mortimer Sturgis, with thirty-eight golfless years behind him, is swept off his feet. He is carried away. He loses all sense of proportion. He is like the fly that happens to be sitting on the wall of the dam just when the crack comes.

Mortimer Sturgis gave himself up without a struggle to an orgy of golf such as I have never witnessed in any man. Within two days of that first lesson he had accumulated a collection of clubs large enough to have enabled him to open a shop; and he went on buying them at the rate of two and three a day. On Sundays, when it was impossible to buy clubs, he was like a lost spirit. True, he would do his regular four rounds on the day of rest, but he never felt happy. The thought, as he sliced into the rough, that the patent wooden-faced cleek which he intended to purchase next morning might have made all the difference, completely spoiled his enjoyment.

I remember him calling me up on the telephone at three o'clock one morning to tell me that he had solved the problem of putting. He intended in future, he said, to use a croquet mallet, and he wondered that no one had ever thought of it before. The sound of his broken groan when I informed him that croquet mallets were against the rules haunted me for days.

His golf library kept pace with his collection of clubs. He bought all the standard works, subscribed to all the golfing papers, and, when he came across a paragraph in a magazine to the effect that Mr Hutchings, an ex-amateur champion, did not begin to play till he was past forty, and that his opponent in the final, Mr S. H. Fry, had never held a club till his thirty-fifth year, he had it engraved on vellum and framed and hung up beside his shaving-mirror.

* * * * * * * * *

And Betty, meanwhile? She, poor child, stared down the years into a bleak future, in which she saw herself parted for ever from the man she loved, and the golf-widow of another for whom – even when he won a medal for lowest net at a weekly handicap with a score of a hundred and three minus twenty-four – she could feel nothing warmer than respect. Those were dreary days for Betty. We three – she and I and Eddie Denton – often talked over Mortimer's strange obsession. Denton said that, except that Mortimer had not come out in pink spots, his symptoms were almost identical with those of the dreaded *mongo-mongo*, the scourge of the West African hinterland. Poor Denton! He had already booked his passage for Africa, and spent hours looking in the atlas for good deserts.

In every fever of human affairs there comes at last the crisis. We may emerge from it healed or we may plunge into still deeper depths of soul-sickness; but always the crisis comes. I was privileged to be present when it came in the affairs of Mortimer Sturgis and Betty Weston.

I had gone into the club-house one afternoon at an hour when it is usually empty, and the first thing I saw, as I entered the main room, which looks out on the ninth green, was Mortimer. He was grovelling on the floor, and I confess that, when I caught sight of him, my heart stood still. I feared that his reason, sapped by dissipation, had given way. I knew that for weeks, day in and day out, the niblick had hardly ever been out of his hand, and no constitution can stand that.

He looked up as he heard my footstep.

'Hallo,' he said. 'Can you see a ball anywhere?'

'A ball?' I backed away, reaching for the door-handle. 'My dear boy,' I said, soothingly, 'you have made a mistake. Quite a natural mistake. One anybody would have made. But, as a matter of fact, this is the club-house. The links are outside there. Why not come away with me very quietly and let us see if we can't find some balls on the links? If you will wait here a moment, I will call up Doctor Smithson. He was telling me only this morning that he wanted a good spell of ball-hunting to put him in shape. You don't mind if he joins us?'

'It was a Silver King with my initials on it,' Mortimer went on, not heeding me. 'I got on the ninth green in eleven with a nice mashie-niblick, but my approach-putt was a little too strong. It came in through that window.'

I perceived for the first time that one of the windows facing the course was broken, and my relief was great. I went down on my knees and helped him in his search. We ran the ball to earth finally inside the piano.

'What's the local rule?' inquired Mortimer. 'Must I play it where it lies, or may I tee up and lose a stroke? If I have to play it where it lies, I suppose a niblick would be the club?'

It was at this moment that Betty came in. One glance at her pale, set face told me that there was to be a scene, and I would have retired, but that she was between me and the door.

'Hallo, dear,' said Mortimer, greeting her with a friendly waggle of his niblick. 'I'm bunkered in the piano. My approach-putt was a little strong, and I over-ran the green.'

'Mortimer,' said the girl, tensely, 'I want to ask you one question.'

'Yes, dear? I wish, darling, you could have seen my drive at the eighth just now. It was a pip!'

Betty looked at him steadily.

'Are we engaged,' she said, 'or are we not?'

'Engaged? Oh, to be married? Why, of course. I tried the open stance for a change, and—'

'This morning you promised to take me for a ride. You never appeared. Where were you?'

'Just playing golf.'

'Golf! I'm sick of the very name!'

A spasm shook Mortimer.

'You mustn't let people hear you saying things like that!' he said. 'I somehow felt, the moment I began my up-swing, that everything was going to be all right. I—'

'I'll give you one more chance. Will you take me for a drive in your car this evening?'

'I can't.'

'Why not? What are you doing?'

'Just playing golf!'

'I'm tired of being neglected like this!' cried Betty, stamping her foot. Poor girl, I saw her point of view. It was bad enough for her being engaged to the wrong man, without having him treat her as a mere acquaintance. Her conscience fighting with her love for Eddie Denton had kept her true to Mortimer, and Mortimer accepted the sacrifice with an absent-minded carelessness which would have been galling to any girl. 'We might just as well not be engaged at all. You never take me anywhere.'

'I asked you to come with me to watch the Open Championship.'

'Why don't you ever take me to dances?'

'I can't dance.'

'You could learn.'

'But I'm not sure if dancing is a good thing for a fellow's game. You never hear of any first-class pro. dancing. James Braid doesn't dance.'

'Well, my mind's made up. Mortimer, you must choose between golf and me.'

'But, darling, I went round in a hundred and one yesterday. You can't expect a fellow to give up golf when he's at the top of his game.'

'Very well. I have nothing more to say. Our engagement is at an end.'

'Don't throw me over, Betty,' pleaded Mortimer, and there was that in his voice which cut me to the heart. 'You'll make me so miserable. And, when I'm miserable, I always slice my approach-shots.'

Betty Weston drew herself up. Her face was hard.

'Here is your ring!' she said, and swept from the room.

* * * * * * * * *

For a moment after she had gone Mortimer remained very still, looking at the glistening circle in his hand. I stole across the room and patted his shoulder.

'Bear up, my boy, bear up!' I said.

He looked at me piteously.

'Stymied!' he muttered.

'Be brave!'

He went on, speaking as if to himself.

'I had pictured – ah, how often I had pictured! – our little home! Hers and mine. She sewing in her arm-chair, I practising putts on the hearth-rug—' He choked. 'While in the corner, little Harry Vardon Sturgis played with little J. H. Taylor Sturgis. And round the room – reading, busy with their childish tasks – little George Duncan Sturgis, Abe Mitchell Sturgis, Harold Hilton Sturgis, Edward Ray Sturgis, Horace Hutchinson Sturgis, and little James Braid Sturgis.'

'My boy! My boy!' I cried.

'What's the matter?'

'Weren't you giving yourself rather a large family?'

He shook his head moodily.

'Was I?' he said, dully. 'I don't know. What's bogey?'

There was a silence.

'And yet—' he said, at last, in a low voice. He paused. An odd, bright look had come into his eyes. He seemed suddenly to be himself again, the old, happy Mortimer Sturgis I had known so well. 'And yet,' he said, 'who knows? Perhaps it is all for the best. They might all have turned out tennis-players!' He raised his niblick again, his face aglow. 'Playing thirteen!' he said. 'I think the game here would be to chip out through the door and work round the club-house to the green, don't you?'

* * * * * * * * *

Little remains to be told. Betty and Eddie have been happily married for years. Mortimer's handicap is now down to eighteen, and he is improving all the time. He was not present at the wedding, being unavoidably detained by a medal tournament; but, if you turn up the files and look at the list of presents, which were both numerous and costly, you will see – somewhere in the middle of the column, the words: –

STURGIS, J. MORTIMER.

Two dozen Silver King Golf-balls and one patent Sturgis Aluminium Self-Adjusting, Self-Compensating Putting-Cleek.

4 SUNDERED HEARTS

In the smoking-room of the club-house a cheerful fire was burning, and the Oldest Member glanced from time to time out of the window into the gathering dusk. Snow was falling lightly on the links. From where he sat, the Oldest Member had a good view of the ninth green; and presently, out of the greyness of the December evening, there appeared over the brow of the hill a golf-ball. It trickled across the green, and stopped within a yard of the hole. The Oldest Member nodded approvingly. A good approach-shot.

A young man in a tweed suit clambered on to the green, holed out with easy confidence, and, shouldering his bag, made his way to the club-house. A few moments later he entered the smoking-room, and uttered an exclamation of rapture at the sight of the fire.

'I'm frozen stiff!'

He rang for a waiter and ordered a hot drink. The Oldest Member gave a gracious assent to the suggestion that he should join him.

'I like playing in winter,' said the young man. 'You get the course to yourself, for the world is full of slackers who only turn out when the weather suits them. I cannot understand where they get the nerve to call themselves golfers.'

'Not everyone is as keen as you are, my boy,' said the Sage, dipping gratefully into his hot drink. 'If they were, the world would be a better place, and we should hear less of all this modern unrest.'

'I *am* pretty keen,' admitted the young man.

'I have only encountered one man whom I could describe as keener. I allude to Mortimer Sturgis.'

'The fellow who took up golf at thirty-eight and let the girl he was engaged to marry go off with someone else because he hadn't the time to combine golf with courtship? I remember. You were telling me about him the other day.'

'There is a sequel to that story, if you would care to hear it,' said the Oldest Member.

'You have the honour,' said the young man. 'Go ahead!'

* * * * * * * * *

Some people (began the Oldest Member) considered that Mortimer Sturgis was too wrapped up in golf, and blamed him for it. I could never see eye to eye with them. In the days of King Arthur nobody thought the worse of a young knight if he suspended all his social and business engagements in favour of a search for the Holy Grail. In the Middle Ages a man could devote his whole life to the Crusades, and the public fawned upon him. Why, then, blame the man of to-day for a zealous attention to the modern equivalent, the Quest of Scratch? Mortimer Sturgis never became a scratch player, but he did eventually get his handicap down to nine, and I honour him for it.

The story which I am about to tell begins in what might be called the middle period of Sturgis's career. He had reached the stage when his handicap was a wobbly twelve; and, as you are no doubt aware, it is then that a man really begins to golf in the true sense of the word. Mortimer's fondness for the game until then had been merely tepid compared with what it now became. He had played a little before, but now he really buckled to and got down to it. It was at this point, too, that he began once more to entertain thoughts of marriage. A profound statistician in this one department, he had discovered that practically all the finest exponents of the art are married men; and the thought that there might be something in the holy state which improved a man's game, and that he was missing a good thing, troubled him a great deal. Moreover, the paternal instinct had awakened in him. As he justly pointed out, whether marriage improved your game or not, it was to Old Tom Morris's marriage that the existence of young Tommy Morris, winner of the British Open Championship four times in succession, could be directly traced. In fact, at the age of forty-two, Mortimer Sturgis was in just the frame of mind to take some nice girl aside and ask her to become a step-mother to his eleven drivers, his baffy, his twenty-eight putters, and the rest of the ninety-four clubs which he had accumulated in the course of his golfing career. The sole stipulation, of course, which he made when dreaming his day-dreams was that the future Mrs Sturgis must be a golfer. I can still recall the horror in his face when one girl, admirable in other respects, said that she had never heard of Harry Vardon, and didn't he mean Dolly Varden? She has since proved an excellent wife and mother, but Mortimer Sturgis never spoke to her again.

With the coming of January, it was Mortimer's practice to leave England and go to the South of France, where there was sunshine and crisp dry turf. He pursued his usual custom this year. With his suit-case and his ninety-four clubs he went off to Saint Brüle, staying as he always did at the Hotel Superbe, where they knew him, and treated with an amiable tolerance his habit of practising chip-shots in his bedroom. On the first evening, after breaking a statuette of the Infant Samuel in Prayer, he dressed and went down to dinner. And the first thing he saw was Her.

Mortimer Sturgis, as you know, had been engaged before, but Betty Weston had never inspired the tumultuous rush of emotion which the mere sight of this girl had set loose in him. He told me later that just to watch her holing out her soup gave him a sort of feeling you get when your drive collides with a rock in the middle of a tangle of rough and kicks back into the middle of the fairway. If golf had come late in life to Mortimer Sturgis, love came later still, and just as the golf, attacking him in middle life, had been some golf, so was the love considerable love. Mortimer finished his dinner in a trance, which is the best way to do it at some hotels, and then scoured the place for someone who would introduce him. He found such a person eventually and the meeting took place.

* * * * * * * * *

She was a small and rather fragile-looking girl, with big blue eyes and a cloud of golden hair. She had a sweet expression, and her left wrist was in a sling. She looked up at Mortimer as if she had at last found something that amounted to something. I am inclined to think it was a case of love at first sight on both sides.

'Fine weather we're having,' said Mortimer, who was a capital conversationalist.

'Yes,' said the girl.

'I like fine weather.'

'So do I.'

'There's something about fine weather!'

'Yes.'

'It's – it's – well, fine weather's so much finer than weather that isn't fine,' said Mortimer.

He looked at the girl a little anxiously, fearing he might be taking her out of her depth, but she seemed to have followed his train of thought perfectly.

'Yes, isn't it?' she said. 'It's so – so fine.'

'That's just what I meant,' said Mortimer. 'So fine. You've just hit it.'

He was charmed. The combination of beauty with intelligence is so rare.

'I see you've hurt your wrist,' he went on, pointing to the sling.

'Yes. I strained it a little playing in the championship.'

'The championship?' Mortimer was interested. 'It's awfully rude of me,' he said, apologetically, 'but I didn't catch your name just now.'

'My name is Somerset.'

Mortimer had been bending forward solicitously. He overbalanced and nearly fell off his chair. The shock had been stunning. Even before he had met and spoken to her, he had told himself that he loved this girl with the stored-up love of a lifetime. And she was Mary Somerset! The hotel lobby danced before Mortimer's eyes.

The name will, of course, be familiar to you. In the early rounds of the Ladies' Open Golf Championship of that year nobody had paid much attention to Mary Somerset. She had survived her first two matches, but her opponents had been nonentities like herself. And then, in the third round, she had met and defeated the champion. From that point on, her name was on everybody's lips. She became favourite. And she had justified the public confidence by sailing into the final and winning easily. And here she was, talking to him like an ordinary person, and, if he could read the message in her eyes, not altogether indifferent to his charms, if you could call them that.

'Golly!' said Mortimer, awed.

* * * * * * * * *

Their friendship ripened rapidly, as friendships do in the South of France. In that favoured clime, you find the girl and Nature does the rest. On the second morning of their acquaintance Mortimer invited her to walk round the links with him and watch him play. He did it a little diffidently, for his golf was not of the calibre that would be likely to extort admiration from a champion. On the other hand, one should never let slip the opportunity of acquiring wrinkles on the game, and he thought that Miss Somerset, if she watched one or two of his shots, might tell him just what he ought to do. And sure enough, the opening arrived on the fourth hole, where Mortimer, after a drive which surprised even himself, found his ball in a nasty cuppy lie.

He turned to the girl.

'What ought I to do here?' he asked.

Miss Somerset looked at the ball. She seemed to be weighing the matter in her mind.

'Give it a good hard knock,' she said.

Mortimer knew what she meant. She was advocating a full iron. The only trouble was that, when he tried anything more ambitious than a half-swing, except off the tee, he almost invariably topped. However, he could not fail this wonderful girl, so he swung well back and took a chance. His enterprise was rewarded. The ball flew out of the indentation in the turf as cleanly as though John Henry Taylor had been behind it, and rolled, looking neither to left nor to right, straight for the pin. A few moments later Mortimer Sturgis had holed out one under bogey, and it was only the fear that, having known him for so short a time, she might be startled and refuse him that kept him from proposing then and there. This exhibition of golfing generalship on her part had removed his last doubts. He knew that, if he lived for ever, there could be no other girl in the world for him. With her at his side, what might he not do? He might get his handicap down to six – to three – to scratch – to plus something! Good heavens, why, even the Amateur Championship was not outside the range of possibility. Mortimer Sturgis shook his putter solemnly in the air, and vowed a silent vow that he would win this pearl among women.

Now, when a man feels like that, it is impossible to restrain him long. For a week Mortimer Sturgis's soul sizzled within him: then he could contain himself no longer. One night, at one of the informal dances at the hotel, he drew the girl out on to the moonlit terrace.

'Miss Somerset—' he began, stuttering with emotion like an imperfectly-corked bottle of ginger-beer. 'Miss Somerset – may I call you Mary?'

The girl looked at him with eyes that shone softly in the dim light.

'Mary?' she repeated. 'Why, of course, if you like—'

'If I like!' cried Mortimer. 'Don't you know that it is my dearest wish? Don't you know that I would rather be permitted to call you Mary than do the first hole at Muirfield in two? Oh, Mary, how I have longed for this moment! I love you! I love you! Ever since I met you I have known that you were the one girl in this vast world whom I would die to win! Mary, will you be mine? Shall we go round together? Will you fix up a match with me on the links of life which shall end only when the Grim Reaper lays us both a stymie?'

She drooped towards him.

'Mortimer!' she murmured.

He held out his arms, then drew back. His face had grown suddenly tense, and there were lines of pain about his mouth.

'Wait!' he said, in a strained voice. 'Mary, I love you dearly, and because I love you so dearly I cannot let you trust your sweet life to me blindly. I have a confession to make. I am not – I have not always been' – he paused – 'a good man,' he said, in a low voice.

She started indignantly.

'How can you say that? You are the best, the kindest, the bravest man I have ever met! Who but a good man would have risked his life to save me from drowning?'

'Drowning?' Mortimer's voice seemed perplexed. 'You? What do you mean?'

'Have you forgotten the time when I fell in the sea last week, and you jumped in with all your clothes on—'

'Of course, yes,' said Mortimer. 'I remember now. It was the day I did the long seventh in five. I got off a good tee-shot straight down the fairway, took a baffy for my second, and— But that is not the point. It is sweet and generous of you to think so highly of what was the merest commonplace act of ordinary politeness, but I must repeat that, judged by the standards of your snowy purity, I am not a good man. I do not come to you clean and spotless as a young girl should expect her husband to come to her. Once, playing in a foursome, my ball fell in some long grass. Nobody was near me. We had no caddies, and the others were on the fairway. God knows—' His voice shook. 'God knows I struggled against the temptation. But I fell.

I kicked the ball on to a little bare mound, from which it was an easy task with a nice half-mashie to reach the green for a snappy seven. Mary, there have been times when, going round by myself, I have allowed myself ten-foot putts on three holes in succession, simply in order to be able to say I had done the course in under a hundred. Ah! you shrink from me! You are disgusted!'

'I'm not disgusted! And I don't shrink! I only shivered because it is rather cold.'

'Then you can love me in spite of my past?'

'Mortimer!'

She fell into his arms.

'My dearest,' he said, presently, 'what a happy life ours will be. That is, if you do not find that you have made a mistake.'

'A mistake!' she cried, scornfully.

'Well, my handicap is twelve, you know, and not so darned twelve at that. There are days when I play my second from the fairway of the next hole but one, days when I couldn't putt into a coal-hole with "Welcome!" written over it. And you are a Ladies' Open Champion. Still, if you think it's all right— Oh, Mary, you little know how I have dreamed of some day marrying a really first-class golfer! Yes, that was my vision – of walking up the aisle with some sweet plus two girl on my arm. You shivered again. You are catching cold.'

'It is a little cold,' said the girl. She spoke in a small voice.

'Let me take you in, sweetheart,' said Mortimer. 'I'll just put you in a comfortable chair with a nice cup of coffee, and then I think I really must come out again and tramp about and think how perfectly splendid everything is.'

* * * * * * * * *

They were married a few weeks later, very quietly, in the little village church of Saint Brüle. The secretary of the local golf-club acted as best man for Mortimer, and a girl from the hotel was the only bridesmaid. The whole business was rather a disappointment to Mortimer, who had planned out a somewhat florid ceremony at St George's, Hanover Square, with the Vicar of Tooting (a scratch player excellent at short approach-shots) officiating, and 'The Voice That Breathed O'er St Andrews' booming from the organ. He had even had the idea of copying the military wedding and escorting his bride out of the church under an arch of crossed cleeks. But she would have none of this pomp. She insisted on a quiet wedding, and for the honeymoon trip preferred a tour through Italy. Mortimer, who had wanted to go to Scotland to visit the birthplace of James Braid, yielded amiably, for he loved her dearly. But he did not think much of Italy. In Rome, the great monuments of the past left him cold. Of the Temple of Vespasian, all he thought was that it would be a devil of a place to be bunkered behind. The Colosseum aroused a faint spark of interest in him, as he speculated whether Abe Mitchell would use a full brassey to carry it. In Florence, the view over the Tuscan Hills from the Torre Rosa, Fuesole, over which his bride waxed enthusiastic, seemed to him merely a nasty bit of rough which would take a deal of getting out of.

And so, in the fullness of time, they came home to Mortimer's cosy little house adjoining the links.

* * * * * * * * *

Mortimer was so busy polishing his ninety-four clubs on the evening of their arrival that he failed to notice that his wife was preoccupied. A less busy man would have perceived at a glance that she was distinctly nervous. She started at sudden noises, and once, when he tried the newest of his mashie-niblicks and broke one of the drawing-room windows, she screamed sharply. In short her manner was strange, and, if Edgar Allan Poe had put her into 'The Fall of the House of Usher', she would have fitted it like the paper on the wall. She had the air of one waiting tensely for the approach of some imminent doom. Mortimer, humming gaily to himself as he sand-papered the blade of his twenty-second putter, observed nothing of this. He was thinking of the morrow's play.

'Your wrist's quite well again now, darling, isn't it?' he said.

'Yes. Yes, quite well.'

'Fine!' said Mortimer. 'We'll breakfast early – say at half-past seven – and then we'll be able to get in a couple of rounds before lunch. A couple more in the afternoon will about see us through. One doesn't want to over-golf oneself the first day.' He swung the putter joyfully. 'How had we better play do you think? We might start with you giving me a half.'

She did not speak. She was very pale. She clutched the arm of her chair tightly till the knuckles showed white under the skin.

To anybody but Mortimer her nervousness would have been even more obvious on the following morning, as they reached the first tee. Her eyes were dull and heavy, and she started when a grasshopper chirruped. But Mortimer was too occupied with thinking how jolly it was having the course to themselves to notice anything.

He scooped some sand out of the box, and took a ball out of her bag. His wedding-present to her had been a brand-new golf-bag, six dozen balls, and a full set of the most expensive clubs, all born in Scotland.

'Do you like a high tee?' he asked.

'Oh, no,' she replied, coming with a start out of her thoughts. 'Doctors say it's indigestible.'

Mortimer laughed merrily.

'Deuced good!' he chuckled. 'Is that your own or did you read it in a comic paper? There you are!' He placed the ball on a little hill of sand, and got up. 'Now let's see some of that championship form of yours!'

She burst into tears.

'My darling!'

Mortimer ran to her and put his arms round her. She tried weakly to push him away.

'My angel! What is it?'

She sobbed brokenly. Then, with an effort, she spoke.

'Mortimer, I have deceived you!'

'Deceived me?'

'I have never played golf in my life! I don't even know how to hold the caddie!'

Mortimer's heart stood still. This sounded like the gibberings of an unbalanced mind, and no man likes his wife to begin gibbering immediately after the honeymoon.

'My precious! You are not yourself!'

'I am! That's the whole trouble! I'm myself and not the girl you thought I was!'

Mortimer stared at her, puzzled. He was thinking that it was a little difficult and that, to work it out properly, he would need a pencil and a bit of paper.

'My name is not Mary!'

'But you said it was.'

'I didn't. You asked if you could call me Mary, and I said you might, because I loved you too much to deny your smallest whim. I was going on to say that it wasn't my name, but you interrupted me.'

'Not Mary!' The horrid truth was coming home to Mortimer. 'You were not Mary Somerset?'

'Mary is my cousin. My name is Mabel.'

'But you said you had sprained your wrist playing in the championship.'

'So I had. The mallet slipped in my hand.'

'The mallet!' Mortimer clutched at his forehead. 'You didn't say "the mallet"?'

'Yes, Mortimer! The mallet!'

A faint blush of shame mantled her cheek, and into her blue eyes there came a look of pain, but she faced him bravely.

'I am the Ladies' Open Croquet Champion!' she whispered.

Mortimer Sturgis cried aloud, a cry that was like the shriek of some wounded animal.

'Croquet!' He gulped, and stared at her with unseeing eyes. He was no prude, but he had those decent prejudices of which no self-respecting man can wholly rid himself, however broad-minded he may try to be. 'Croquet!'

There was a long silence. The light breeze sang in the pines above them. The grasshoppers chirruped at their feet.

She began to speak again in a low, monotonous voice.

'I blame myself! I should have told you before, while there was yet time for you to withdraw. I should have confessed this to you that night on the terrace in the moonlight. But you swept me off my feet, and I was in your arms before I realized what you would think of me. It was only then that I understood what my supposed skill at golf meant to you, and then it was too late. I loved you too much to let you go! I could not bear the thought of you recoiling from me. Oh, I was mad – mad! I knew that I could not keep up the deception for ever, that you must find me out in time. But I had a wild hope that by then we should be so close to one another that you might find it in your heart to forgive. But I was wrong. I see it now. There are some things that no man can forgive. Some things,' she repeated, dully, 'which no man can forgive.'

She turned away. Mortimer awoke from his trance.

'Stop!' he cried. 'Don't go!'

'I must go.'

'I want to talk this over.'

She shook her head sadly and started to walk slowly across the sunlit grass. Mortimer watched her, his brain in a whirl of chaotic thoughts. She disappeared through the trees.

Mortimer sat down on the tee-box, and buried his face in his hands. For a time he could think of nothing but the cruel blow he had received. This was the end of those rainbow visions of himself and her going through life side by side, she lovingly criticizing his stance and his back-swing, he learning wisdom from her. A croquet-player! He was married to a woman who hit coloured balls through hoops. Mortimer Sturgis writhed in torment. A strong man's agony.

The mood passed. How long it had lasted, he did not know. But suddenly, as he sat there, he became once more aware of the glow of the sunshine and the singing of the birds. It was as if a shadow had lifted. Hope and optimism crept into his heart.

He loved her. He loved her still. She was part of him, and nothing that she could do had power to alter that. She had deceived him, yes. But why had she deceived him? Because she loved him so much that she could not bear to lose him. Dash it all, it was a bit of a compliment.

And, after all, poor girl, was it her fault? Was it not rather the fault of her upbringing? Probably she had been taught to play croquet when a mere child, hardly able to distinguish right from wrong. No steps had been taken to eradicate the virus from her system, and the thing had become chronic. Could she be blamed? Was she not more to be pitied than censured?

Mortimer rose to his feet, his heart swelling with generous forgiveness. The black horror had passed from him. The future seemed once more bright. It was not too late. She was still young, many years younger than he himself had been when he took up golf, and surely, if she put herself into the hands of a good specialist and practised every day, she might still hope to become a fair player. He reached the house and ran in, calling her name.

No answer came. He sped from room to room, but all were empty.

She had gone. The house was there. The furniture was there. The canary sang in its cage, the cook in the kitchen. The pictures still hung on the walls. But she had gone. Everything was at home except his wife.

Finally, propped up against the cup he had once won in a handicap competition, he saw a letter. With a sinking heart he tore open the envelope.

It was a pathetic, a tragic letter, the letter of a woman endeavouring to express all the anguish of a torn heart with one of those fountain-pens which suspend the flow of ink about twice in every three words. The gist of it was that she felt she had wronged him; that, though he might forgive, he could never forget; and that she was going away, away out into the world alone.

Mortimer sank into a chair, and stared blankly before him. She had scratched the match.

* * * * * * * * *

I am not a married man myself, so have had no experience of how it feels to have one's wife whizz off silently into the unknown; but I should imagine that it must be something like taking a full swing with a brassey and missing the ball. Something, I take it, of the same sense of mingled shock, chagrin, and the feeling that nobody loves one, which attacks a man in such circumstances, must come to the bereaved husband. And one can readily understand how terribly the incident must have shaken Mortimer Sturgis. I was away at the time, but I am told by those who saw him that his game went all to pieces.

He had never shown much indication of becoming anything in the nature of a first-class golfer, but he had managed to acquire one or two decent shots. His work with the light iron was not at all bad, and he was a fairly steady putter. But now, under the shadow of this tragedy, he dropped right back to the form of his earliest period. It was a pitiful sight to see this gaunt, haggard man with the look of dumb anguish behind his spectacles taking as many as three shots sometimes to get past the ladies' tee. His slice, of which he had almost cured himself, returned with such virulence that in the list of ordinary hazards he had now to include the tee-box. And, when he was not slicing, he was pulling. I have heard that he was known, when driving at the sixth, to get bunkered in his own caddie, who had taken up his position directly behind him. As for the deep sand-trap in front of the seventh green, he spent so much of his time in it that there was some informal talk among the members of the committee of charging him a small weekly rent.

A man of comfortable independent means, he lived during these days on next to nothing. Golf-balls cost him a certain amount, but the bulk of his income he spent in efforts to discover his wife's whereabouts. He advertised in all the papers. He employed private detectives. He even, much as it revolted his finer instincts, took to travelling about the country, watching croquet matches. But she was never among the players. I am not sure that he did not find a melancholy comfort in this, for it seemed to show that, whatever his wife might be and whatever she might be doing, she had not gone right under.

Summer passed. Autumn came and went. Winter arrived. The days grew bleak and chill, and an early fall of snow, heavier than had been known at that time of the year for a long while, put an end to golf. Mortimer spent his days indoors, staring gloomily through the window at the white mantle that covered the earth.

It was Christmas Eve.

* * * * * * * * *

The young man shifted uneasily on his seat. His face was long and sombre.

'All this is very depressing,' he said.

'These soul tragedies,' agreed the Oldest Member, 'are never very cheery.'

'Look here,' said the young man, firmly, 'tell me one thing frankly, as man to man. Did Mortimer find her dead in the snow, covered except for her face, on which still lingered that faint, sweet smile which he remembered so well? Because, if he did, I'm going home.'

'No, no,' protested the Oldest Member. 'Nothing of that kind.'

'You're sure? You aren't going to spring it on me suddenly?'

'No, no!'

The young man breathed a relieved sigh.

'It was your saying that about the white mantle covering the earth that made me suspicious.'

The Sage resumed.

* * * * * * * * *

It was Christmas Eve. All day the snow had been falling, and now it lay thick and deep over the countryside. Mortimer Sturgis, his frugal dinner concluded – what with losing his wife and not being able to get any golf, he had little appetite these days – was sitting in his drawing-room, moodily polishing the blade of his jigger. Soon wearying of this once congenial task, he laid down the club and went to the front door, to see if there was any chance of a thaw. But no. It was freezing. The snow, as he tested it with his shoe, crackled crisply. The sky above was black and full of cold stars. It seemed to Mortimer that the sooner he packed up and went to the South of France, the better. He was just about to close the door, when suddenly he thought he heard his own name called.

'Mortimer!'

Had he been mistaken? The voice had sounded faint and far away.

'Mortimer!'

He thrilled from head to foot. This time there could be no mistake. It was the voice he knew so well, his wife's voice, and it had come from somewhere down near the garden-gate. It is difficult to judge distance where sounds are concerned, but Mortimer estimated that the voice had spoken about a short mashie-niblick and an easy putt from where he stood.

The next moment he was racing down the snow-covered path. And then his heart stood still. What was that dark something on the ground just inside the gate? He leaped towards it. He passed his hands over it. It was a human body. Quivering, he struck a match. It went out. He struck another. That went out, too. He struck a third, and it burnt with a steady flame; and, stooping, he saw that it was his wife who lay there, cold and stiff. Her eyes were closed, and on her face still lingered that faint, sweet smile which he remembered so well.

* * * * * * * * *

The young man rose with a set face. He reached for his golf-bag.

'I call that a dirty trick,' he said, 'after you promised—' The Sage waved him back to his seat.

'Have no fear! She had only fainted.'

'You said she was cold.'

'Wouldn't you be cold if you were lying in the snow?'

'And stiff.'

'Mrs Sturgis was stiff because the train-service was bad, it being the holiday-season, and she had had to walk all the way from the junction, a distance of eight miles. Sit down and allow me to proceed.'

* * * * * * * * *

Tenderly, reverently Mortimer Sturgis picked her up and began to bear her into the house. Half-way there, his foot slipped on a piece of ice and he fell heavily, barking his shin and shooting his lovely burden out on to the snow.

The fall brought her to. She opened her eyes.

'Mortimer, darling!' she said.

Mortimer had just been going to say something else, but he checked himself.

'Are you alive?' he asked.

'Yes,' she replied.

'Thank God!' said Mortimer, scooping some of the snow out of the back of his collar.

Together they went into the house, and into the drawing-room. Wife gazed at husband, husband at wife. There was a silence.

'Rotten weather!' said Mortimer.

'Yes, isn't it!'

The spell was broken. They fell into each other's arms. And presently they were sitting side by side on the sofa, holding hands, just as if that awful parting had been but a dream.

It was Mortimer who made the first reference to it.

'I say, you know,' he said, 'you oughtn't to have nipped away like that!'

'I thought you hated me!'

'Hated *you*! I love you better than life itself! I would sooner have smashed my pet driver than have had you leave me!'

She thrilled at the words.

'Darling!'

Mortimer fondled her hand.

'I was just coming back to tell you that I loved you still. I was going to suggest that you took lessons from some good professional. And I found you gone!'

'I wasn't worthy of you, Mortimer!'

'My angel!' He pressed his lips to her hair, and spoke solemnly. 'All this has taught me a lesson, dearest. I knew all along, and I know it more than ever now, that it is you – you that I want. Just you! I don't care if you don't play golf. I don't care—' He hesitated, then went on manfully. 'I don't care even if you play croquet, so long as you are with me!'

For a moment her face showed a rapture that made it almost angelic. She uttered a low moan of ecstasy. She kissed him. Then she rose.

'Mortimer, look!'

'What at?'

'Me. Just look!'

The jigger which he had been polishing lay on a chair close by. She took it up. From the bowl of golf-balls on the mantelpiece she selected a brand-new one. She placed it on the carpet. She addressed it. Then, with a merry cry of 'Fore!' she drove it hard and straight through the glass of the china-cupboard.

'Good God!' cried Mortimer, astounded. It had been a bird of a shot.

She turned to him, her whole face alight with that beautiful smile.

'When I left you, Mortie,' she said, 'I had but one aim in life, somehow to make myself worthy of you. I saw your advertisements in the papers, and I longed to answer them, but I was not ready. All this long, weary while I have been in the village of Auchtermuchtie, in Scotland, studying under Tammas McMickle.'

'Not the Tammas McMickle who finished fourth in the Open Championship of 1911, and had the best ball in the foursome in 1912 with Jock McHaggis, Andy McHeather, and Sandy McHoots!'

'Yes, Mortimer, the very same. Oh, it was difficult at first. I missed my mallet, and longed to steady the ball with my foot and use the toe of the club. Wherever there was a direction post I aimed at it automatically. But I conquered my weakness. I practised steadily. And now Mr McMickle says my handicap would be a good twenty-four on any links.' She smiled apologetically. 'Of course, that doesn't sound much to you! You were a twelve when I left you, and now I suppose you are down to eight or something.'

Mortimer shook his head.

'Alas, no!' he replied, gravely. 'My game went right off for some reason or other, and I'm twenty-four, too.'

'For some reason or other!' She uttered a cry. 'Oh, I know what the reason was! How can I ever forgive myself! I have ruined your game!'

The brightness came back to Mortimer's eyes. He embraced her fondly.

'Do not reproach yourself, dearest,' he murmured. 'It is the best thing that could have happened. From now on, we start level, two hearts that beat as one, two drivers that drive as one. I could not wish it otherwise. By George! It's just like that thing of Tennyson's.'

He recited the lines softly: –

My bride,
My wife, my life. Oh, we will walk the links
Yoked in all exercise of noble end,
And so thro' those dark bunkers off the course
That no man knows. Indeed, I love thee: come,
Yield thyself up: our handicaps are one;
Accomplish thou my manhood and thyself;
Lay thy sweet hands in mine and trust to me.

She laid her hands in his.

'And now, Mortie, darling,' she said, 'I want to tell you all about how I did the long twelfth at Auchtermuchtie in one under bogey.'

5 THE SALVATION OF GEORGE MACKINTOSH

The young man came into the club-house. There was a frown on his usually cheerful face, and he ordered a ginger-ale in the sort of voice which an ancient Greek would have used when asking the executioner to bring on the hemlock.

Sunk in the recesses of his favourite settee the Oldest Member had watched him with silent sympathy.

'How did you get on?' he inquired.

'He beat me.'

The Oldest Member nodded his venerable head.

'You have had a trying time, if I am not mistaken. I feared as much when I saw you go out with Pobsley. How many a young man have I seen go out with Herbert Pobsley exulting in his youth, and crawl back at eventide looking like a toad under the harrow! He talked?'

'All the time, confound it! Put me right off my stroke.'

The Oldest Member sighed.

'The talking golfer is undeniably the most pronounced pest of our complex modern civilization,' he said, 'and the most difficult to deal with. It is a melancholy thought that the noblest of games should have produced such a scourge. I have frequently marked Herbert Pobsley in action. As the crackling of thorns under a pot . . . He is almost as bad as poor George Mackintosh in his worst period. Did I ever tell you about George Mackintosh?'

'I don't think so.'

'His,' said the Sage, 'is the only case of golfing garrulity I have ever known where a permanent cure was effected. If you would care to hear about it—?'

* * * * * * * * *

George Mackintosh (said the Oldest Member), when I first knew him, was one of the most admirable young fellows I have ever met. A handsome, well-set-up man, with no vices except a tendency to use the mashie for shots which should have been made with the light iron. And as for his positive virtues, they were too numerous to mention. He never swayed his body, moved his head, or pressed. He was always ready to utter a tactful grunt when his opponent foozled. And when he himself achieved a glaring fluke, his self-reproachful click of the tongue was music to his adversary's bruised soul. But of all his virtues the one that most endeared him to me and to all thinking men was the fact that, from the start of a round to the finish, he never spoke a word except when absolutely compelled to do so by the exigencies of the game. And it was this man who subsequently, for a black period which lives in the memory of all his contemporaries, was known as Gabby George and became a shade less popular than the germ of Spanish Influenza. Truly, *corruptio optimi pessima!*

One of the things that sadden a man as he grows older and reviews his life is the reflection that his most devastating deeds were generally the ones which he did with the best motives. The thought is disheartening. I can honestly say that, when George Mackintosh came to me and told me his troubles, my sole desire was to ameliorate his lot. That I might be starting on the downward path a man whom I liked and respected never once occurred to me.

One night after dinner when George Mackintosh came in, I could see at once that there was something on his mind, but what this could be I was at a loss to imagine, for I had been playing with him myself all the afternoon, and he had done an eighty-one and a seventy-nine. And, as I had not left the links till dusk was beginning to fall, it was practically impossible that he could have gone out again and done badly. The idea of financial trouble seemed equally out of the question. George had a good job with the old-established legal firm of Peabody, Peabody, Peabody, Peabody, Cootes, Toots, and Peabody. The third alternative, that he might be in love, I rejected at once. In all the time I had known him I had never seen a sign that George Mackintosh gave a thought to the opposite sex.

Yet this, bizarre as it seemed, was the true solution. Scarcely had he seated himself and lit a cigar when he blurted out his confession.

'What would you do in a case like this?' he said.

'Like what?'

'Well—' He choked, and a rich blush permeated his surface. 'Well, it seems a silly thing to say and all that, but I'm in love with Miss Tennant, you know!'

'You are in love with Celia Tennant?'

'Of course I am. I've got eyes, haven't I? Who else is there that any sane man could possibly be in love with? That,' he went on, moodily, 'is the whole trouble. There's a field of about twenty-nine, and I should think my place in the betting is about thirty-three to one.'

'I cannot agree with you there,' I said. 'You have every advantage, it appears to me. You are young, amiable, good-looking, comfortably off, scratch—'

'But I can't talk, confound it!' he burst out. 'And how is a man to get anywhere at this sort of game without talking?'

'You are talking perfectly fluently now.'

'Yes, to you. But put me in front of Celia Tennant, and I simply make a sort of gurgling noise like a sheep with the botts. It kills my chances stone dead. You know these other men. I can give Claude Mainwaring a third and beat him. I can give Eustace Brinkley a stroke a hole and simply trample on his corpse. But when it comes to talking to a girl, I'm not in their class.'

'You must not be diffident.'

'But I *am* diffident. What's the good of saying I mustn't be diffident when I'm the man who wrote the words and music, when Diffidence is my middle name and my telegraphic address? I can't help being diffident.'

'Surely you could overcome it?'

'But how? It was in the hope that you might be able to suggest something that I came round to-night.'

And this was where I did the fatal thing. It happened that, just before I took up 'Braid on the Push-Shot', I had been dipping into the current number of a magazine, and one of the advertisements, I chanced to remember, might have been framed with a special eye to George's unfortunate case. It was that one, which I have no doubt you have seen, which treats of 'How to Become a Convincing Talker'. I picked up this magazine now and handed it to George.

He studied it for a few minutes in thoughtful silence. He looked at the picture of the Man who had taken the course being fawned upon by lovely women, while the man who had let this opportunity slip stood outside the group gazing with a wistful envy.

'They never do that to me,' said George.

'Do what, my boy?'

'Cluster round, clinging cooingly.'

'I gather from the letterpress that they will if you write for the booklet.'

'You think there is really something in it?'

'I see no reason why eloquence should not be taught by mail. One seems to be able to acquire every other desirable quality in that manner nowadays.'

'I might try it. After all, it's not expensive. There's no doubt about it,' he murmured, returning to his perusal, 'that fellow does look popular. Of course, the evening dress may have something to do with it.'

'Not at all. The other man, you will notice, is also wearing evening dress, and yet he is merely among those on the outskirts. It is simply a question of writing for the booklet.'

'Sent post free.'

'Sent, as you say, post free.'

'I've a good mind to try it.'

'I see no reason why you should not.'

'I will, by Duncan!' He tore the page out of the magazine and put it in his pocket. 'I'll tell you what I'll do. I'll give this thing a trial for a week or two, and at the end of that time I'll go to the boss and see how he reacts when I ask for a rise of salary. If he crawls, it'll show there's something in this. If he flings me out, it will prove the thing's no good.'

We left it at that, and I am bound to say – owing, no doubt, to my not having written for the booklet of the Memory

Training Course advertised on the adjoining page of the magazine – the matter slipped from my mind. When, therefore, a few weeks later, I received a telegram from young Mackintosh which ran:

Worked like magic,

I confess I was intensely puzzled. It was only a quarter of an hour before George himself arrived that I solved the problem of its meaning.

* * * * * * * * *

'So the boss crawled?' I said, as he came in.

He gave a light, confident laugh. I had not seen him, as I say, for some time, and I was struck by the alteration in his appearance. In what exactly this alteration consisted I could not at first have said; but gradually it began to impress itself on me that his eye was brighter, his jaw squarer, his carriage a trifle more upright than it had been. But it was his eye that struck me most forcibly. The George Mackintosh I had known had had a pleasing gaze, but, though frank and agreeable, it had never been more dynamic than a fried egg. This new George had an eye that was a combination of a gimlet and a searchlight. Coleridge's Ancient Mariner, I imagine, must have been somewhat similarly equipped. The Ancient Mariner stopped a wedding guest on his way to a wedding; George Mackintosh gave me the impression that he could have stopped the Cornish Riviera express on its way to Penzance. Self-confidence – aye, and more than self-confidence – a sort of sinful, overbearing swank seemed to exude from his very pores.

'Crawled?' he said. 'Well, he didn't actually lick my boots, because I saw him coming and side-stepped; but he did everything short of that. I hadn't been talking an hour when—'

'An hour!' I gasped. 'Did you talk for an hour?'

'Certainly. You wouldn't have had me be abrupt, would you? I went into his private office and found him alone. I think at first he would have been just as well pleased if I had retired. In fact, he said as much. But I soon adjusted that outlook. I took a seat and a cigarette, and then I started to sketch out for him the history of my connection with the firm. He began to wilt before the end of the first ten minutes. At the quarter of an hour mark he was looking at me like a lost dog that's just found its owner. By the half-hour he was making little bleating noises and massaging my coat-sleeve. And when, after perhaps an hour and a half, I came to my peroration and suggested a rise, he choked back a sob, gave me double what I had asked, and invited me to dine at his club next Tuesday. I'm a little sorry now I cut the thing so short. A few minutes more, and I fancy he would have given me his sock-suspenders and made over his life-insurance in my favour.'

'Well,' I said, as soon as I could speak, for I was finding my young friend a trifle overpowering, 'this is most satisfactory.'

'So-so,' said George. 'Not un-so-so. A man wants an addition to his income when he is going to get married.'

'Ah!' I said. 'That, of course, will be the real test.'

'What do you mean?'

'Why, when you propose to Celia Tennant. You remember you were saying when we spoke of this before—'

'Oh, that!' said George, carelessly. 'I've arranged all that.'

'What!'

'Oh, yes. On my way up from the station. I looked in on Celia about an hour ago, and it's all settled.'

'Amazing!'

'Well, I don't know. I just put the thing to her, and she seemed to see it.'

'I congratulate you. So now, like Alexander, you have no more worlds to conquer.'

'Well, I don't know so much about that,' said George. 'The way it looks to me is that I'm just starting. This eloquence is a thing that rather grows on one. You didn't hear about my after-dinner speech at the anniversary banquet of the firm, I suppose? My dear fellow, a riot! A positive stampede. Had 'em laughing and then crying and then laughing again and then crying once more till six of 'em had to be led out and the rest down with hiccoughs. Napkins waving . . . three tables broken . . . waiters in hysterics. I tell you, I played on them as on a stringed instrument . . .'

'Can you play on a stringed instrument?'

'As it happens, no. But as I would have played on a stringed instrument if I could play on a stringed instrument. Wonderful sense of power it gives you. I mean to go in pretty largely for that sort of thing in future.'

'You must not let it interfere with your golf.'

He gave a laugh which turned my blood cold.

'Golf!' he said. 'After all, what is golf? Just pushing a small ball into a hole. A child could do it. Indeed, children have done it with great success. I see an infant of fourteen has just won some sort of championship. Could that stripling convulse a roomful of banqueters? I think not! To sway your fellow-men with a word, to hold them with a gesture . . . that is the real salt of life. I don't suppose I shall play much more golf now. I'm making arrangements for a lecturing-tour, and I'm booked up for fifteen lunches already.'

Those were his words. A man who had once done the lake-hole in one. A man whom the committee were grooming for the amateur championship. I am no weakling, but I confess they sent a chill shiver down my spine.

George Mackintosh did not, I am glad to say, carry out his mad project to the letter. He did not altogether sever himself from golf. He was still to be seen occasionally on the links. But now – and I know of nothing more tragic that can befall a man – he found himself gradually shunned, he who in the days of his sanity had been besieged with more offers of games than he could manage to accept. Men simply would not stand his incessant flow of talk. One by one they dropped off, until the only person he could find to go round with him was old Major Moseby, whose hearing completely petered out as long ago as the year '98. And, of course, Celia Tennant would play with him occasionally; but it seemed to me that even she, greatly as no doubt she loved him, was beginning to crack under the strain.

So surely had I read the pallor of her face and the wild look of dumb agony in her eyes that I was not surprised when, as I sat one morning in my garden reading Ray On Taking Turf, my man announced her name. I had been half expecting her to come to me for advice and consolation, for I had known her ever since she was a child. It was I who had given her her first driver and taught her infant lips to lisp 'Fore!' It is not easy to lisp the word 'Fore!' but I had taught her to do it, and this constituted a bond between us which had been strengthened rather than weakened by the passage of time.

She sat down on the grass beside my chair, and looked up at my face in silent pain. We had known each other so long that I know that it was not my face that pained her, but rather some unspoken *malaise* of the soul. I waited for her to speak, and suddenly she burst out impetuously as though she could hold back her sorrow no longer.

'Oh, I can't stand it! I can't stand it!'

'You mean . . . ?' I said, though I knew only too well.

'This horrible obsession of poor George's,' she cried passionately. 'I don't think he has stopped talking once since we have been engaged.'

'He *is* chatty,' I agreed. 'Has he told you the story about the Irishman?'

'Half a dozen times. And the one about the Swede oftener than that. But I would not mind an occasional anecdote. Women have to learn to bear anecdotes from the men they love. It is the curse of Eve. It is his incessant easy flow of chatter on all topics that is undermining even my devotion.'

'But surely, when he proposed to you, he must have given you an inkling of the truth. He only hinted at it when he spoke to me, but I gather that he was eloquent.'

'When he proposed,' said Celia dreamily, 'he was wonderful. He spoke for twenty minutes without stopping. He said I was the essence of his every hope, the tree on which the fruit of his life grew; his Present, his Future, his Past . . . oh, and all that sort of thing. If he would only confine his conversation now to remarks of a similar nature, I could listen to him all day long. But he doesn't. He talks politics and statistics and philosophy and . . . oh, and everything. He makes my head ache.'

'And your heart also, I fear,' I said gravely.

'I love him!' she replied simply. 'In spite of everything, I love him dearly. But what to to? What to do? I have an awful fear that when we are getting married instead of answering

"I will," he will go into the pulpit and deliver an address on Marriage Ceremonies of All Ages. The world to him is a vast lecture-platform. He looks on life as one long after-dinner, with himself as the principal speaker of the evening. It is breaking my heart. I see him shunned by his former friends. Shunned! They run a mile when they see him coming. The mere sound of his voice outside the club-house is enough to send brave men diving for safety beneath the sofas. Can you wonder that I am in despair? What have I to live for?'

'There is always golf.'

'Yes, there is always golf,' she whispered bravely.

'Come and have a round this afternoon.'

'I had promised to go for a walk...' She shuddered, then pulled herself together. '... for a walk with George.'

I hesitated for a moment.

'Bring him along,' I said, and patted her hand. 'It may be that together we shall find an opportunity of reasoning with him.'

She shook her head.

'You can't reason with George. He never stops talking long enough to give you time.'

'Nevertheless, there is no harm in trying. I have an idea that this malady of his is not permanent and incurable. The very violence with which the germ of loquacity has attacked him gives me hope. You must remember that before this seizure he was rather a noticeably silent man. Sometimes I think that it is just Nature's way of restoring the average, and that soon the fever may burn itself out. Or it may be that a sudden shock... At any rate, have courage.'

'I will try to be brave.'

'Capital! At half-past two on the first tee, then.'

'You will have to give me a stroke on the third, ninth, twelfth, fifteenth, sixteenth and eighteenth,' she said, with a quaver in her voice. 'My golf has fallen off rather lately.'

I patted her hand again.

'I understand,' I said gently. 'I understand.'

* * * * * * * * *

The steady drone of a baritone voice as I alighted from my car and approached the first tee told me that George had not forgotten the tryst. He was sitting on the stone seat under the chestnut-tree, speaking a few well-chosen words on the Labour Movement.

'To what conclusion, then, do we come?' he was saying. 'We come to the foregone and inevitable conclusion that . . .'

'Good afternoon, George,' I said.

He nodded briefly, but without verbal salutation. He seemed to regard my remark as he would have regarded the unmannerly heckling of some one at the back of the hall. He proceeded evenly with his speech, and was still talking when Celia addressed her ball and drove off. Her drive, coinciding with a sharp rhetorical question from George, wavered in mid-air, and the ball trickled off into the rough half-way down the hill. I can see the poor girl's tortured face even now. But she breathed no word of reproach. Such is the miracle of woman's love.

'Where you went wrong there,' said George, breaking off his remarks on Labour, 'was that you have not studied the dynamics of golf sufficiently. You did not pivot properly. You allowed your left heel to point down the course when you were at the top of your swing. This makes for instability and loss of distance. The fundamental law of the dynamics of golf is that the left foot shall be solidly on the ground at the moment of impact. If you allow your heel to point down the course, it is almost impossible to bring it back in time to make the foot a solid fulcrum.'

I drove, and managed to clear the rough and reach the fairway. But it was not one of my best drives. George Mackintosh, I confess, had unnerved me. The feeling he gave me resembled the self-conscious panic which I used to experience in my childhood when informed that there was One Awful Eye that watched my every movement and saw my every act. It was only the fact that poor Celia appeared even more affected by his espionage that enabled me to win the first hole in seven.

On the way to the second tee George discoursed on the beauties of Nature, pointing out at considerable length how exquisitely the silver glitter of the lake harmonized with the vivid emerald turf near the hole and the duller green of the rough beyond it. As Celia teed up her ball, he directed her attention to the golden glory of the sand-pit to the left of the flag. It was not the spirit in which to approach the lake-hole, and I was not surprised when the unfortunate girl's ball fell with a sickening plop half-way across the water.

'Where you went wrong there,' said George, 'was that you made the stroke a sudden heave instead of a smooth, snappy flick of the wrists. Pressing is always bad, but with the mashie—'

'I think I will give you this hole,' said Celia to me, for my shot had cleared the water and was lying on the edge of the green. 'I wish I hadn't used a new ball.'

'The price of golf-balls,' said George, as we started to round the lake, 'is a matter to which economists should give some attention. I am credibly informed that rubber at the present time is exceptionally cheap. Yet we see no decrease in the price of golf-balls, which, as I need scarcely inform you, are rubber-cored. Why should this be so? You will say that the wages of skilled labour have gone up. True. But—'

'One moment, George, while I drive,' I said. For we had now arrived at the third tee.

'A curious thing, concentration,' said George, 'and why certain phenomena should prevent us from focusing our attention— This brings me to the vexed question of sleep. Why is it that we are able to sleep through some vast convulsion of Nature when a dripping tap is enough to keep us awake? I am told that there were people who slumbered peacefully through the San Francisco earthquake, merely stirring drowsily from time to time to tell an imaginary person to leave it on the mat. Yet these same people—'

Celia's drive bounded into the deep ravine which yawns some fifty yards from the tee. A low moan escaped her.

'Where you went wrong there—' said George.

'I know,' said Celia. 'I lifted my head.'

I had never heard her speak so abruptly before. Her manner, in a girl less noticeably pretty, might almost have been called snappish. George, however, did not appear to have noticed anything amiss. He filled his pipe and followed her into the ravine.

'Remarkable,' he said, 'how fundamental a principle of golf is this keeping the head still. You will hear professionals tell their pupils to keep their eye on the ball. Keeping the eye on the ball is only a secondary matter. What they really mean is that the head should be kept rigid, as otherwise it is impossible to—'

His voice died away. I had sliced my drive into the woods on the right, and after playing another had gone off to try to find my ball, leaving Celia and George in the ravine behind me. My last glimpse of them showed me that her ball had fallen into a stone-studded cavity in the side of the hill, and she was drawing her niblick from her bag as I passed out of sight. George's voice, blurred by distance to a monotonous murmur, followed me until I was out of earshot.

I was just about to give up the hunt for my ball in despair, when I heard Celia's voice calling to me from the edge of the undergrowth. There was a sharp note in it which startled me.

I came out, trailing a portion of some unknown shrub which had twined itself about my ankle.

'Yes?' I said, picking twigs out of my hair.

'I want your advice,' said Celia.

'Certainly. What is the trouble? By the way,' I said, looking round, 'where is your *fiancé*?'

'I have no *fiancé*,' she said, in a dull, hard voice.

'You have broken off the engagement?'

'Not exactly. And yet – well, I suppose it amounts to that.'

'I don't quite understand.'

'Well, the fact is,' said Celia, in a burst of girlish frankness, 'I rather think I've killed George.'

'Killed him, eh?'

It was a solution that had not occurred to me, but now that it was presented for my inspection I could see its merits. In these days of national effort, when we are all working together to try to make our beloved land fit for heroes to live in, it was astonishing that nobody before had thought of a simple, obvious thing like killing George Mackintosh. George Mackintosh was undoubtedly better dead, but it had taken a woman's intuition to see it.

'I killed him with my niblick,' said Celia.

I nodded. If the thing was to be done at all, it was unquestionably a niblick shot.

'I had just made my eleventh attempt to get out of that ravine,' the girl went on, 'with George talking all the time about the recent excavations in Egypt, when suddenly – you know what it is when something seems to snap—'

'I had the experience with my shoe-lace only this morning.'

'Yes, it was like that. Sharp – sudden – happening all in a moment. I suppose I must have said something, for George stopped talking about Egypt and said that he was reminded by a remark of the last speaker's of a certain Irishman—'

I pressed her hand.

'Don't go on if it hurts you,' I said, gently.

'Well, there is very little more to tell. He bent his head to light his pipe, and well – the temptation was too much for me. That's all.'

'You were quite right.'

'You really think so?'

'I certainly do. A rather similar action, under far less provocation, once made Jael the wife of Heber the most popular woman in Israel.'

'I wish I could think so too,' she murmured. 'At the moment, you know, I was conscious of nothing but an awful elation. But – but – oh, he was such a darling before he got this dreadful affliction. I can't help thinking of G-George as he used to be.'

She burst into a torrent of sobs.

'Would you care for me to view the remains?' I said.

'Perhaps it would be as well.'

She led me silently into the ravine. George Mackintosh was lying on his back where he had fallen.

'There!' said Celia.

And, as she spoke, George Mackintosh gave a kind of snorting groan and sat up. Celia uttered a sharp shriek and sank on her knees before him. George blinked once or twice and looked about him dazedly.

'Save the women and children!' he cried. 'I can swim.'

'Oh, George!' said Celia.

'Feeling a little better?' I asked.

'A little. How many people were hurt?'

'Hurt?'

'When the express ran into us.' He cast another glance around him. 'Why, how did I get here?'

'You were here all the time,' I said.

'Do you mean after the roof fell in or before?'

Celia was crying quietly down the back of his neck.

'Oh, George!' she said, again.

He groped out feebly for her hand and patted it.

'Brave little woman!' he said. 'Brave little woman! She stuck by me all through. Tell me – I am strong enough to bear it – what caused the explosion?'

It seemed to me a case where much unpleasant explanation might be avoided by the exercise of a little tact.

'Well, some say one thing and some another,' I said. 'Whether it was a spark from a cigarette—'

Celia interrupted me. The woman in her made her revolt against this well-intentioned subterfuge.

'I hit you, George!'

'Hit me?' he repeated, curiously. 'What with? The Eiffel Tower?'

'With my niblick.'

'You hit me with your niblick? But why?'

She hesitated. Then she faced him bravely.

'Because you wouldn't stop talking.'

He gaped.

'Me!' he said. '*I* wouldn't stop talking! But I hardly talk at all. I'm noted for it.'

Celia's eyes met mine in agonized inquiry. But I saw what had happened. The blow, the sudden shock, had operated on George's brain-cells in such a way as to effect a complete cure. I have not the technical knowledge to be able to explain it, but the facts were plain.

'Lately, my dear fellow,' I assured him, 'you have dropped into the habit of talking rather a good deal. Ever since we started out this afternoon you have kept up an incessant flow of conversation!'

'Me! On the links! It isn't possible.'

'It is only too true, I fear. And that is why this brave girl hit you with her niblick. You started to tell her a funny story just as she was making her eleventh shot to get her ball out of this ravine, and she took what she considered the necessary steps.'

'Can you ever forgive me, George?' cried Celia.

George Mackintosh stared at me. Then a crimson blush mantled his face.

'So I did! It's all beginning to come back to me. Oh, heavens!'

'*Can* you forgive me, George?' cried Celia again.

He took her hand in his.

'Forgive you?' he muttered. 'Can *you* forgive *me*? Me – a tee-talker, a green-gabbler, a prattler on the links, the lowest form of life known to science! I am unclean, unclean!'

'It's only a little mud, dearest,' said Celia, looking at the sleeve of his coat. 'It will brush off when it's dry.'

'How can you link your lot with a man who talks when people are making their shots?'

'You will never do it again.'

'But I have done it. And you stuck to me all through! Oh, Celia!'

'I loved you, George!'

The man seemed to swell with a sudden emotion. His eyes lit up, and he thrust one hand into the breast of his coat while he raised the other in a sweeping gesture. For an instant he appeared on the verge of a flood of eloquence. And then, as if he had been made sharply aware of what it was that he intended to do, he suddenly sagged. The gleam died out of his eyes. He lowered his hand.

'Well, I must say that was rather decent of you,' he said.

A lame speech, but one that brought an infinite joy to both his hearers. For it showed that George Mackintosh was cured beyond possibility of relapse.

'Yes, I must say you are rather a corker,' he added.

'George!' cried Celia.

I said nothing, but I clasped his hand; and then, taking my clubs, I retired. When I looked round she was still in his arms. I left them there, alone together in the great silence.

* * * * * * * * *

And so (concluded the Oldest Member) you see that a cure is possible, though it needs a woman's gentle hand to bring it about. And how few women are capable of doing what Celia Tennant did. Apart from the difficulty of summoning up the necessary resolution, an act like hers requires a straight eye and a pair of strong and supple wrists. It seems to me that for the ordinary talking golfer there is no hope. And the race seems to be getting more numerous every day. Yet the finest golfers are always the least loquacious. It is related of the illustrious Sandy McHoots that when, on the occasion of his winning the British Open Championship, he was interviewed by reporters from the leading daily papers as to his views on Tariff Reform, Bimetallism, the Trial by Jury System, and the Modern Craze for Dancing, all they could extract from him was the single word 'Mphm!' Having uttered which, he shouldered his bag and went home to tea. A great man. I wish there were more like him.

6 ORDEAL BY GOLF

A pleasant breeze played among the trees on the terrace outside the Marvis Bay Golf and Country Club. It ruffled the leaves and cooled the forehead of the Oldest Member, who, as was his custom of a Saturday afternoon, sat in the shade on a rocking-chair, observing the younger generation as it hooked and sliced in the valley below. The eye of the Oldest Member was thoughtful and reflective. When it looked into yours you saw in it that perfect peace, that peace beyond understanding, which comes at its maximum only to the man who has given up golf.

The Oldest Member has not played golf since the rubber-cored ball superseded the old dignified gutty. But as a spectator and philosopher he still finds pleasure in the pastime. He is watching it now with keen interest. His gaze, passing from the lemonade which he is sucking through a straw, rests upon the Saturday foursome which is struggling raggedly up the hill to the ninth green. Like all Saturday foursomes, it is in difficulties. One of the patients is zigzagging about the fairway like a liner pursued by submarines. Two others seem to be digging for buried treasure, unless – it is too far off to be certain – they are killing snakes. The remaining cripple, who has just foozled a mashie-shot, is blaming his caddie. His voice, as he upbraids the innocent child for breathing during his up-swing, comes clearly up the hill.

The Oldest Member sighs. His lemonade gives a sympathetic gurgle. He puts it down on the table.

* * * * * * * * *

How few men, says the Oldest Member, possess the proper golfing temperament! How few indeed, judging by the sights I see here on Saturday afternoons, possess any qualification at all for golf except a pair of baggy knickerbockers and enough money to enable them to pay for the drinks at the end of the round. The ideal golfer never loses his temper. When I played, I never lost my temper. Sometimes, it is true, I may, after missing a shot, have broken my club across my knees; but I did it in a calm and judicial spirit, because the club was obviously no good and I was going to get another one anyway. To lose one's temper at golf is foolish. It gets you nothing, not even relief. Imitate the spirit of Marcus Aurelius. 'Whatever may befall thee,' says that great man in his 'Meditations', 'it was preordained for thee from everlasting. Nothing happens to anybody which he is not fitted by nature to bear.' I like to think that this noble thought came to him after he had sliced a couple of new balls into the woods, and that he jotted it down on the back of his score-card. For there can be no doubt that the man was a golfer, and a bad golfer at that. Nobody who had not had a short putt stop on the edge of the hole could possibly have written the words: 'That which makes the man no worse than he was makes life no worse. It has no power to harm, without or within.' Yes, Marcus Aurelius undoubtedly played golf, and all the evidence seems to indicate that he rarely went round in under a hundred and twenty. The niblick was his club.

Speaking of Marcus Aurelius and the golfing temperament recalls to my mind the case of young Mitchell Holmes. Mitchell, when I knew him first, was a promising young man with a future before him in the Paterson Dyeing and Refining Company, of which my old friend, Alexander Paterson, was the president. He had many engaging qualities – among them an unquestioned ability to imitate a bulldog quarrelling with a Pekingese in a way which had to be heard to be believed. It was a gift which made him much in demand at social gatherings in the neighbourhood, marking him off from other young men who could only almost play the mandolin or recite bits of Gunga Din; and no doubt it was this talent of his which first sowed the seeds of love in the heart of Millicent Boyd. Women are essentially hero-worshippers, and when a warm-hearted girl like Millicent has heard a personable young man imitating a bulldog and a Pekingese to the applause of a crowded drawing-room, and has been able to detect the exact point at which the Pekingese leaves off and the bulldog begins, she can never feel quite the same to other men. In short, Mitchell and Millicent were engaged, and were only waiting to be married till the former could bite the Dyeing and Refining Company's ear for a bit of extra salary.

Mitchell Holmes had only one fault. He lost his temper when playing golf. He seldom played a round without becoming piqued, peeved, or – in many cases – chagrined. The caddies on our links, it was said, could always worst other small boys in verbal argument by calling them some of the things they had heard Mitchell call his ball on discovering it in a cuppy lie. He had a great gift of language, and he used it unsparingly. I will admit that there was some excuse for the man. He had the makings of a brilliant golfer, but a combination of bad luck and inconsistent play invariably robbed him of the fruits of his skill. He was the sort of player who does the first two holes in one under bogey and then takes an eleven at the third. The least thing upset him on the links. He missed short putts because of the uproar of the butterflies in the adjoining meadows.

It seemed hardly likely that this one kink in an otherwise admirable character would ever seriously affect his working or professional life, but it did. One evening, as I was sitting in my garden, Alexander Paterson was announced. A glance at his face told me that he had come to ask my advice. Rightly or wrongly, he regarded me as one capable of giving advice. It was I who had changed the whole current of his life by counselling him to leave the wood in his bag and take a driving-iron off the tee; and in one or two other matters, like the choice of a putter (so much more important than the choice of a wife), I had been of assistance to him.

Alexander sat down and fanned himself with his hat, for the evening was warm. Perplexity was written upon his fine face.

'I don't know what to do,' he said.

'Keep the head still – slow back – don't press,' I said, gravely. There is no better rule for a happy and successful life.

'It's nothing to do with golf this time,' he said. 'It's about the treasurership of my company. Old Smithers retires next week, and I've got to find a man to fill his place.'

'That should be easy. You have simply to select the most deserving from among your other employees.'

'But which *is* the most deserving? That's the point. There are two men who are capable of holding the job quite adequately. But then I realize how little I know of their real characters. It is the treasurership, you understand, which has to be filled. Now, a man who was quite good at another job might easily get wrong ideas into his head when he became a treasurer. He would have the handling of large sums of money. In other words, a man who in ordinary circumstances had never been conscious of any desire to visit the more distant portions of South America might feel the urge, so to speak, shortly after he became a treasurer. That is my difficulty. Of course, one always takes a sporting chance with any treasurer; but how am I to find out which of these two men would give me the more reasonable opportunity of keeping some of my money?'

I did not hesitate a moment. I held strong views on the subject of character-testing.

'The only way,' I said to Alexander, 'of really finding out a man's true character is to play golf with him. In no other walk of life does the cloven hoof so quickly display itself. I employed a lawyer for years, until one day I saw him kick his ball out of a heel-mark. I removed my business from his charge next morning. He has not yet run off with any trust-funds, but there is a nasty gleam in his eye, and I am convinced that it is only a question of time. Golf, my dear fellow, is the infallible test. The man who can go into a patch of rough alone, with the knowledge that only God is watching him, and play his ball where it lies, is the man who will serve you faithfully and well. The man who can smile bravely when his putt is diverted by one of those beastly worm-casts is pure gold right through. But the man who is hasty, unbalanced, and violent on the links will display the same qualities in the wider field of everyday life. You don't want an unbalanced treasurer do you?'

'Not if his books are likely to catch the complaint.'

'They are sure to. Statisticians estimate that the average of crime among good golfers is lower than in any class of the community except possibly bishops. Since Willie Park won the first championship at Prestwick in the year 1860 there has, I believe, been no instance of an Open Champion spending a day in prison. Whereas the bad golfers – and by bad I do not mean incompetent, but black-souled – the men who fail to count a stroke when they miss the globe; the men who never replace a divot; the men who talk while their opponent is driving; and the men who let their angry passions rise – these are in and out of Wormwood Scrubbs all the time. They find it hardly worth while to get their hair cut in their brief intervals of liberty.'

Alexander was visibly impressed.

'That sounds sensible, by George!' he said.

'It is sensible.'

'I'll do it! Honestly, I can't see any other way of deciding between Holmes and Dixon.'

I started.

'Holmes? Not Mitchell Holmes?'

'Yes. Of course you must know him? He lives here, I believe.'

'And by Dixon do you mean Rupert Dixon?'

'That's the man. Another neighbour of yours.'

I confess that my heart sank. It was as if my ball had fallen into the pit which my niblick had digged. I wished heartily that I had thought of waiting to ascertain the names of the two rivals before offering my scheme. I was extremely fond of Mitchell Holmes and of the girl to whom he was engaged to be married. Indeed, it was I who had sketched out a few rough notes for the lad to use when proposing; and results had shown that he had put my stuff across well. And I had listened many a time with a sympathetic ear to his hopes in the matter of securing a rise of salary which would enable him to get married. Somehow, when Alexander was talking, it had not occurred to me that young Holmes might be in the running for so important an office as the treasurership. I had ruined the boy's chances. Ordeal by golf was the one test which he could not possibly undergo with success. Only a miracle could keep him from losing his temper, and I had expressly warned Alexander against such a man.

When I thought of his rival my heart sank still more. Rupert Dixon was rather an unpleasant young man, but the worst of his enemies could not accuse him of not possessing the golfing temperament. From the drive off the tee to the holing of the final putt he was uniformly suave.

* * * * * * * * *

When Alexander had gone, I sat in thought for some time. I was faced with a problem. Strictly speaking, no doubt, I had no right to take sides; and, though secrecy had not been enjoined upon me in so many words, I was very well aware that Alexander was under the impression that I would keep the thing under my hat and not reveal to either party the test that awaited him. Each candidate was, of course, to remain ignorant that he was taking part in anything but a friendly game.

But when I thought of the young couple whose future depended on this ordeal, I hesitated no longer. I put on my hat and went round to Miss Boyd's house, where I knew that Mitchell was to be found at this hour.

The young couple were out in the porch, looking at the moon. They greeted me heartily, but their heartiness had rather a tinny sound, and I could see that on the whole they regarded me as one of those things which should not happen. But when I told my story their attitude changed. They began to look on me in the pleasanter light of a guardian, philosopher, and friend.

'Wherever did Mr Paterson get such a silly idea?' said Miss Boyd, indignantly. I had – from the best motives – concealed the source of the scheme. 'It's ridiculous!'

'Oh, I don't know,' said Mitchell. 'The old boy's crazy about golf. It's just the sort of scheme he would cook up. Well, it dishes *me*!'

'Oh, come!' I said.

'It's no good saying "Oh, come!" You know perfectly well that I'm a frank, outspoken golfer. When my ball goes off nor'-nor'-east when I want it to go due west I can't help expressing an opinion about it. It is a curious phenomenon which calls for comment, and I give it. Similarly, when I top my drive, I have to go on record as saying that I did not do it intentionally. And it's just these trifles, as far as I can make out, that are going to decide the thing.'

'Couldn't you learn to control yourself on the links, Mitchell, darling?' asked Millicent. 'After all, golf is only a game!'

Mitchell's eyes met mine, and I have no doubt that mine showed just the same look of horror which I saw in his. Women say these things without thinking. It does not mean that there is any kink in their character. They simply don't realize what they are saying.

'Hush!' said Mitchell, huskily, patting her hand and overcoming his emotion with a strong effort. 'Hush, dearest!'

* * * * * * * * *

Two or three days later I met Millicent coming from the post-office. There was a new light of happiness in her eyes, and her face was glowing.

'Such a splendid thing has happened,' she said. 'After Mitchell left that night I happened to be glancing through a magazine, and I came across a wonderful advertisement. It began by saying that all the great men in history owed their success to being able to control themselves, and that Napoleon wouldn't have amounted to anything if he had not curbed his fiery nature, and then it said that we can all be like Napoleon if we fill in the accompanying blank order-form for Professor Orlando Rollitt's wonderful book, "Are You Your Own Master?" absolutely free for five days and then seven shillings, but you must write at once because the demand is enormous and pretty soon it may be too late. I wrote at once, and luckily I was in time, because Professor Rollitt did have a copy left, and it's just arrived. I've been looking through it, and it seems splendid.'

She held out a small volume. I glanced at it. There was a frontispiece showing a signed photograph of Professor Orlando Rollitt controlling himself in spite of having long white whiskers, and then some reading matter, printed between wide margins. One look at the book told me the professor's methods. To be brief, he had simply swiped Marcus Aurelius's best stuff, the copyright having expired some two thousand years ago, and was retailing it as his own. I did not mention this to Millicent. It was no affair of mine. Presumably, however obscure the necessity, Professor Rollitt had to live.

'I'm going to start Mitchell on it to-day. Don't you think this is good? "Thou seest how few be the things which if a man has at his command his life flows gently on and is divine." I think it will be wonderful if Mitchell's life flows gently on and is divine for seven shillings, don't you?'

* * * * * * * * *

At the club-house that evening I encountered Rupert Dixon. He was emerging from a shower-bath, and looked as pleased with himself as usual.

'Just been going round with old Paterson,' he said. 'He was asking after you. He's gone back to town in his car.'

I was thrilled. So the test had begun!

'How did you come out?' I asked.

Rupert Dixon smirked. A smirking man, wrapped in a bath towel, with a wisp of wet hair over one eye, is a repellent sight.

'Oh, pretty well. I won by six and five. In spite of having poisonous luck.'

I felt a gleam of hope at these last words.

'Oh, you had bad luck?'

'The worst. I over-shot the green at the third with the best brassey-shot I've ever made in my life – and that's saying a lot – and lost my ball in the rough beyond it.'

'And I suppose you let yourself go, eh?'

'Let myself go?'

'I take it that you made some sort of demonstration?'

'Oh, no. Losing your temper doesn't get you anywhere at golf. It only spoils your next shot.'

I went away heavy-hearted. Dixon had plainly come through the ordeal as well as any man could have done. I expected to hear every day that the vacant treasurership had been filled, and that Mitchell had not even been called upon to play his test round. I suppose, however, that Alexander Paterson felt that it would be unfair to the other competitor not to give him his chance, for the next I heard of the matter was when Mitchell Holmes rang me up on the Friday and asked me if I would accompany him round the links next day in the match he was playing with Alexander, and give him my moral support.

'I shall need it,' he said. 'I don't mind telling you I'm pretty nervous. I wish I had had longer to get the strangle-hold on that "Are You Your Own Master?" stuff. I can see, of course, that it is the real tabasco from start to finish, and absolutely as mother makes it, but the trouble is I've only had a few days to soak it into my system. It's like trying to patch up a motor car with string.

You never know when the thing will break down. Heaven knows what will happen if I sink a ball at the water-hole. And something seems to tell me I am going to do it.'

There was silence for a moment.

'Do you believe in dreams?' asked Mitchell.

'Believe in what?'

'Dreams.'

'What about them?'

'I said, "Do you believe in dreams?" Because last night I dreamed that I was playing in the final of the Open Championship, and I got into the rough, and there was a cow there, and the cow looked at me in a sad sort of way and said, "Why don't you use the two-V grip instead of the interlocking?" At the time it seemed an odd sort of thing to happen, but I've been thinking it over and I wonder if there isn't something in it. These things must be sent to us for a purpose.'

'You can't change your grip on the day of an important match.'

'I suppose not. The fact is, I'm a bit jumpy, or I wouldn't have mentioned it. Oh, well! See you to-morrow at two.'

* * * * * * * * *

The day was bright and sunny, but a tricky cross-wind was blowing when I reached the club-house. Alexander Paterson was there, practising swings on the first tee; and almost immediately Mitchell Holmes arrived, accompanied by Millicent.

'Perhaps,' said Alexander, 'we had better be getting under way. Shall I take the honour?'

'Certainly,' said Mitchell.

Alexander teed up his ball.

Alexander Paterson has always been a careful rather than a dashing player. It is his custom, a sort of ritual, to take two measured practice-swings before addressing the ball, even on the putting-green. When he does address the ball he shuffles his feet for a moment or two, then pauses, and scans the horizon in a suspicious sort of way, as if he had been expecting it to play some sort of a trick on him when he was not looking. A careful inspection seems to convince him of the horizon's *bona fides*, and he turns his attention to the ball again. He shuffles his feet once more, then raises his club. He waggles the club smartly over the ball three times, then lays it behind the globule. At this point he suddenly peers at the horizon again, in the apparent hope of catching it off its guard. This done, he raises his club very slowly, brings it back very slowly till it almost touches the ball, raises it again, brings it down again, raises it once more, and brings it down for the third time. He then stands motionless, wrapped in thought, like some Indian fakir contemplating the infinite. Then he raises his club again and replaces it behind the ball. Finally he quivers all over, swings very slowly back, and drives the ball for about a hundred and fifty yards in a dead straight line.

It is a method of procedure which proves sometimes a little exasperating to the highly strung, and I watched Mitchell's face anxiously to see how he was taking his first introduction to it. The unhappy lad had blenched visibly. He turned to me with the air of one in pain.

'Does he always do that?' he whispered.

'Always,' I replied.

'Then I'm done for! No human being could play golf against a one-ring circus like that without blowing up!'

I said nothing. It was, I feared, only too true. Well-poised as I am, I had long since been compelled to give up playing with Alexander Paterson, much as I esteemed him. It was a choice between that and resigning from the Baptist Church.

At this moment Millicent spoke. There was an open book in her hand. I recognized it as the life-work of Professor Rollitt.

'Think on this doctrine,' she said, in her soft, modulated voice, 'that to be patient is a branch of justice, and that men sin without intending it.'

Mitchell nodded briefly, and walked to the tee with a firm step.

'Before you drive, darling,' said Millicent, 'remember this. Let no act be done at haphazard, nor otherwise than according to the finished rules that govern its kind.'

The next moment Mitchell's ball was shooting through the air, to come to rest two hundred yards down the course. It was a magnificent drive. He had followed the counsel of Marcus Aurelius to the letter.

An admirable iron-shot put him in reasonable proximity to the pin, and he holed out in one under bogey with one of the nicest putts I have ever beheld. And when at the next hole, the dangerous water-hole, his ball soared over the pond and lay safe, giving him bogey for the hole, I began for the first time to breathe freely. Every golfer has his day, and this was plainly Mitchell's. He was playing faultless golf. If he could continue in this vein, his unfortunate failing would have no chance to show itself.

The third hole is long and tricky. You drive over a ravine – or possibly into it. In the latter event you breathe a prayer and call for your niblick. But, once over the ravine, there is nothing to disturb the equanimity. Bogey is five, and a good drive, followed by a brassey-shot, will put you within easy mashie-distance of the green.

Mitchell cleared the ravine by a hundred and twenty yards. He strolled back to me, and watched Alexander go through his ritual with an indulgent smile. I knew just how he was feeling. Never does the world seem so sweet and fair and the foibles of our fellow-human beings so little irritating as when we have just swatted the pill right on the spot.

'I can't see why he does it,' said Mitchell, eyeing Alexander with a toleration that almost amounted to affection. 'If I did all those Swedish exercises before I drove, I should forget what I had come out for and go home.' Alexander concluded the movements, and landed a bare three yards on the other side of the ravine. 'He's what you would call a steady performer, isn't he? Never varies!'

Mitchell won the hole comfortably. There was a jauntiness about his stance on the fourth tee which made me a little uneasy. Over-confidence at golf is almost as bad as timidity.

My apprehensions were justified. Mitchell topped his ball. It rolled twenty yards into the rough, and nestled under a dock-leaf. His mouth opened, then closed with a snap. He came over to where Millicent and I were standing.

'I didn't say it!' he said. 'What on earth happened then?'

'Search men's governing principles,' said Millicent, 'and consider the wise, what they shun and what they cleave to.'

'Exactly,' I said. 'You swayed your body.'

'And now I've got to go and look for that infernal ball.'

'Never mind, darling,' said Millicent. 'Nothing has such power to broaden the mind as the ability to investigate systematically and truly all that comes under thy observation in life.'

'Besides,' I said, 'you're three up.'

'I shan't be after this hole.'

He was right. Alexander won it in five, one above bogey, and regained the honour.

Mitchell was a trifle shaken. His play no longer had its first careless vigour. He lost the next hole, halved the sixth, lost the short seventh, and then, rallying, halved the eighth.

The ninth hole, like so many on our links, can be a perfectly simple four, although the rolling nature of the green makes bogey always a somewhat doubtful feat; but, on the other hand, if you foozle your drive, you can easily achieve double figures. The tee is on the farther side of the pond, beyond the bridge, where the water narrows almost to the dimensions of a brook. You drive across this water and over a tangle of trees and undergrowth on the other bank. The distance to the fairway cannot be more than sixty yards, for the hazard is purely a mental one, and yet how many fair hopes have been wrecked there!

Alexander cleared the obstacles comfortably with his customary short, straight drive, and Mitchell advanced to the tee.

I think the loss of the honour had been preying on his mind. He seemed nervous. His up-swing was shaky, and he swayed back perceptibly. He made a lunge at the ball, sliced it, and it struck a tree on the other side of the water and fell in the long grass. We crossed the bridge to look for it; and it was here that the effect of Professor Rollitt began definitely to wane.

'Why on earth don't they mow this darned stuff?' demanded Mitchell, querulously, as he beat about the grass with his niblick.

'You have to have rough on a course,' I ventured.

'Whatever happens at all,' said Millicent, 'happens as it should. Thou wilt find this true if thou shouldst watch narrowly.'

'That's all very well,' said Mitchell, watching narrowly in a clump of weeds but seeming unconvinced. 'I believe the Greens Committee run this bally club purely in the interests of the caddies. I believe they encourage lost balls, and go halves with the little beasts when they find them and sell them!'

Millicent and I exchanged glances. There were tears in her eyes.

'Oh, Mitchell! Remember Napoleon!'

'Napoleon! What's Napoleon got to do with it? Napoleon never was expected to drive through a primeval forest. Besides, what did Napoleon ever do? Where did Napoleon get off, swanking round as if he amounted to something? Poor fish! All he ever did was to get hammered at Waterloo!'

Alexander rejoined us. He had walked on to where his ball lay.

'Can't find it, eh? Nasty bit of rough, this!'

'No, I can't find it. But to-morrow some miserable, chinless, half-witted reptile of a caddie with pop eyes and eight hundred and thirty-seven pimples will find it, and will sell it to someone for sixpence! No, it was a brand-new ball. He'll probably get a shilling for it. That'll be sixpence for himself and sixpence for the Greens Committee. No wonder they're buying cars quicker than the makers can supply them. No wonder you see their wives going about in mink coats and pearl necklaces. Oh, dash it! I'll drop another!'

'In that case,' Alexander pointed out, 'you will, of course, under the rules governing matchplay, lose the hole.'

'All right, then. I'll give up the hole.'

'Then that, I think, makes me one up on the first nine,' said Alexander. 'Excellent! A very pleasant, even game.'

'Pleasant! On second thoughts I don't believe the Greens Committee let the wretched caddies get any of the loot. They hang round behind trees till the deal's concluded, and then sneak out and choke it out of them!'

I saw Alexander raise his eyebrows. He walked up the hill to the next tee with me.

'Rather a quick-tempered young fellow, Holmes!' he said, thoughtfully. 'I should never have suspected it. It just shows how little one can know of a man, only meeting him in business hours.'

I tried to defend the poor lad.

'He has an excellent heart, Alexander. But the fact is – we are such old friends that I know you will forgive my mentioning it – your style of play gets, I fancy, a little on his nerves.'

'My style of play? What's wrong with my style of play?'

'Nothing is actually wrong with it, but to a young and ardent spirit there is apt to be something a trifle upsetting in being compelled to watch a man play quite so slowly as you do. Come now, Alexander, as one friend to another, is it necessary to take two practice-swings before you putt?'

'Dear, dear!' said Alexander. 'You really mean to say that that upsets him? Well, I'm afraid I am too old to change my methods now.'

I had nothing more to say.

As we reached the tenth tee, I saw that we were in for a few minutes' wait. Suddenly I felt a hand on my arm. Millicent was standing beside me, dejection written on her face. Alexander and young Mitchell were some distance away from us.

'Mitchell doesn't want me to come round the rest of the way with him,' she said, despondently. 'He says I make him nervous.'

I shook my head.

'That's bad! I was looking on you as a steadying influence.'

'I thought I was, too. But Mitchell says no. He says my being there keeps him from concentrating.'

'Then perhaps it would be better for you to remain in the club-house till we return. There is, I fear, dirty work ahead.'

A choking sob escaped the unhappy girl.

'I'm afraid so. There is an apple tree near the thirteenth hole, and Mitchell's caddie is sure to start eating apples. I am thinking of what Mitchell will do when he hears the crunching when he is addressing his ball.'

'That is true.'

'Our only hope,' she said, holding out Professor Rollitt's book, 'is this. Will you please read him extracts when you see him getting nervous? We went through the book last night and marked all the passages in blue pencil which might prove helpful. You will see notes against them in the margin, showing when each is supposed to be used.'

It was a small favour to ask. I took the book and gripped her hand silently. Then I joined Alexander and Mitchell on the tenth tee. Mitchell was still continuing his speculations regarding the Greens Committee.

'The hole after this one,' he said, 'used to be a short hole. There was no chance of losing a ball. Then, one day, the wife of one of the Greens Committee happened to mention that the baby needed new shoes, so now they've tacked on another hundred and fifty yards to it. You have to drive over the brow of a hill, and if you slice an eighth of an inch you get into a sort of No Man's Land, full of rocks and bushes and crevices and old pots and pans. The Greens Committee practically live there in the summer. You see them prowling round in groups, encouraging each other with merry cries as they fill their sacks. Well, I'm going to fool them to-day. I'm going to drive an old ball which is just hanging together by a thread. It'll come to pieces when they pick it up!'

Golf, however, is a curious game – a game of fluctuations. One might have supposed that Mitchell, in such a frame of mind, would have continued to come to grief. But at the beginning of the second nine he once more found his form. A perfect drive put him in position to reach the tenth green with an iron-shot, and, though the ball was several yards from the hole, he laid it dead with his approach-putt and holed his second for a bogey four. Alexander could only achieve a five, so that they were all square again.

The eleventh, the subject of Mitchell's recent criticism, is certainly a tricky hole, and it is true that a slice does land the player in grave difficulties. To-day, however, both men kept their drives straight, and found no difficulty in securing fours.

'A little more of this,' said Mitchell, beaming, 'and the Greens Committee will have to give up piracy and go back to work.'

The twelfth is a long, dog-leg hole, bogey five. Alexander plugged steadily round the bend, holing out in six, and Mitchell, whose second shot had landed him in some long grass, was obliged to use his niblick. He contrived, however, to halve the hole with a nicely-judged mashie-shot to the edge of the green.

Alexander won the thirteenth. It is a three-hundred-and-sixty-yard hole, free from bunkers. It took Alexander three strokes to reach the green, but his third laid the ball dead; while Mitchell, who was on in two, required three putts.

'That reminds me,' said Alexander, chattily, 'of a story I heard. Friend calls out to a beginner, "How are you getting on, old man?" and the beginner says, "Splendidly. I just made three perfect putts on the last green!"'

Mitchell did not appear amused. I watched his face anxiously. He had made no remark, but the missed putt which would have saved the hole had been very short, and I feared the worst.

There was a brooding look in his eye as we walked to the fourteenth tee.

There are few more picturesque spots in the whole of the countryside than the neighbourhood of the fourteenth tee. It is a sight to charm the nature-lover's heart.

But, if golf has a defect, it is that it prevents a man being a whole-hearted lover of nature. Where the layman sees waving grass and romantic tangles of undergrowth, your golfer beholds nothing but a nasty patch of rough from which he must divert his ball. The cry of the birds, wheeling against the sky, is to the golfer merely something that may put him off his putt. As a spectator, I am fond of the ravine at the bottom of the slope. It pleases the eye. But, as a golfer, I have frequently found it the very devil.

The last hole had given Alexander the honour again. He drove even more deliberately than before. For quite half a minute he stood over his ball, pawing at it with his driving-iron like a cat investigating a tortoise. Finally he despatched it to one of the few safe spots on the hillside. The drive from this tee has to be carefully calculated, for, if it be too straight, it will catch the slope and roll down into the ravine.

Mitchell addressed his ball. He swung up, and then, from immediately behind him came a sudden sharp crunching sound. I looked quickly in the direction whence it came. Mitchell's caddie, with a glassy look in his eyes, was gnawing a large apple. And even as I breathed a silent prayer, down came the driver, and the ball, with a terrible slice on it, hit the side of the hill and bounded into the ravine.

There was a pause – a pause in which the world stood still. Mitchell dropped his club and turned. His face was working horribly.

'Mitchell!' I cried. 'My boy! Reflect! Be calm!'

'Calm! What's the use of being calm when people are chewing apples in thousands all round you? What *is* this, anyway – a golf match or a pleasant day's outing for the children of the poor? Apples! Go on, my boy, take another bite. Take several. Enjoy yourself! Never mind if it seems to cause me a fleeting annoyance. Go on with your lunch! You probably had a light breakfast, eh, and are feeling a little peckish, yes? If you will wait here, I will run to the club-house and get you a sandwich and a bottle of ginger-ale. Make yourself quite at home, you lovable little fellow! Sit down and have a good time!'

I turned the pages of Professor Rollitt's book feverishly. I could not find a passage that had been marked in blue pencil to meet this emergency. I selected one at random.

'Mitchell,' I said, 'one moment. How much time he gains who does not look to see what his neighbour says or does, but only at what he does himself, to make it just and holy.'

'Well, look what I've done myself! I'm somewhere down at the bottom of that dashed ravine, and it'll take me a dozen strokes to get out. Do you call that just and holy? Here, give me that book for a moment!'

He snatched the little volume out of my hands. For an instant he looked at it with a curious expression of loathing, then he placed it gently on the ground and jumped on it a few times. Then he hit it with his driver. Finally, as if feeling that the time for half measures had passed, he took a little run and kicked it strongly into the long grass.

He turned to Alexander, who had been an impassive spectator of the scene.

'I'm through!' he said. 'I concede the match. Good-bye. You'll find me in the bay!'

'Going swimming?'

'No. Drowning myself.'

A gentle smile broke out over my old friend's usually grave face. He patted Mitchell's shoulder affectionately.

'Don't do that, my boy,' he said. 'I was hoping you would stick around the office awhile as treasurer of the company.'

Mitchell tottered. He grasped my arm for support. Everything was very still. Nothing broke the stillness but the humming of the bees, the murmur of the distant wavelets, and the sound of Mitchell's caddie going on with his apple.

'What!' cried Mitchell.

'The position,' said Alexander, 'will be falling vacant very shortly, as no doubt you know. It is yours, if you care to accept it.'

'You mean – you mean – you're going to give me the job?'

'You have interpreted me exactly.'

Mitchell gulped. So did his caddie. One from a spiritual, the other from a physical cause.

'If you don't mind excusing me,' said Mitchell, huskily, 'I think I'll be popping back to the club-house. Someone I want to see.'

He disappeared through the trees, running strongly. I turned to Alexander.

'What does this mean?' I asked. 'I am delighted, but what becomes of the test?'

My old friend smiled gently.

'The test,' he replied, 'has been eminently satisfactory. Circumstances, perhaps, have compelled me to modify the original idea of it, but nevertheless it has been a completely successful test. Since we started out, I have been doing a good deal of thinking, and I have come to the conclusion that what the Paterson Dyeing and Refining Company really needs is a treasurer whom I can beat at golf. And I have discovered the ideal man. Why,' he went on, a look of holy enthusiasm on his fine old face, 'do you realize that I can always lick the stuffing out of that boy, good player as he is, simply by taking a little trouble? I can make him get the wind up every time, simply by taking one or two extra practice-swings! That is the sort of man I need for a responsible post in my office.'

'But what about Rupert Dixon?' I asked.

He gave a gesture of distaste.

'I wouldn't trust that man. Why, when I played with him, everything went wrong, and he just smiled and didn't say a word. A man who can do that is not the man to trust with the control of large sums of money. It wouldn't be safe. Why, the fellow isn't honest! He can't be.' He paused for a moment. 'Besides,' he added, thoughtfully, 'he beat me by six and five. What's the good of a treasurer who beats the boss by six and five?'

7 THE LONG HOLE

The young man, as he sat filling his pipe in the club-house smoking-room, was inclined to be bitter.

'If there's one thing that gives me a pain squarely in the centre of the gizzard,' he burst out, breaking a silence that had lasted for some minutes, 'it's a golf-lawyer. They oughtn't to be allowed on the links.'

The Oldest Member, who had been meditatively putting himself outside a cup of tea and a slice of seed-cake, raised his white eyebrows.

'The Law,' he said, 'is an honourable profession. Why should its practitioners be restrained from indulgence in the game of games?'

'I don't mean actual lawyers,' said the young man, his acerbity mellowing a trifle under the influence of tobacco. 'I mean the blighters whose best club is the book of rules. You know the sort of excrescences. Every time you think you've won a hole, they dig out Rule eight hundred and fifty-three, section two, sub-section four, to prove that you've disqualified yourself by having an ingrowing toe-nail. Well, take my case.' The young man's voice was high and plaintive. 'I go out with that man Hemming-way to play an ordinary friendly round – nothing depending on it except a measly ball – and on the seventh he pulls me up and claims the hole simply because I happened to drop my niblick in the bunker. Oh, well, a tick's a tick, and there's nothing more to say, I suppose.'

The Sage shook his head.

'Rules are rules, my boy, and must be kept. It is odd that you should have brought up this subject, for only a moment before you came in I was thinking of a somewhat curious match which ultimately turned upon a question of the rule-book. It is true that, as far as the actual prize was concerned, it made little difference. But perhaps I had better tell you the whole story from the beginning.'

The young man shifted uneasily in his chair.

'Well, you know, I've had a pretty rotten time this afternoon already—'

'I will call my story,' said the Sage, tranquilly, '"The Long Hole", for it involved the playing of what I am inclined to think must be the longest hole in the history of golf. In its beginnings the story may remined you of one I once told you about Peter Willard and James Todd, but you will find that it develops in quite a different manner. Ralph Bingham . . .'

'I half promised to go and see a man—'

'But I will begin at the beginning,' said the Sage. 'I see that you are all impatience to hear the full details.'

* * * * * * * * *

Ralph Bingham and Arthur Jukes (said the Oldest Member) had never been friends – their rivalry was too keen to admit of that – but it was not till Amanda Trivett came to stay here that a smouldering distaste for each other burst out into the flames of actual enmity. It is ever so. One of the poets, whose name I cannot recall, has a passage, which I am unable at the moment to remember, in one of his works, which for the time being has slipped my mind, which hits off admirably this age-old situation. The gist of his remarks is that lovely woman rarely fails to start something. In the weeks that followed her arrival, being in the same room with the two men was like dropping in on a reunion of Capulets and Montagues.

You see, Ralph and Arthur were so exactly equal in their skill on the links that life for them had for some time past resolved itself into a silent, bitter struggle in which first one, then the other, gained some slight advantage. If Ralph won the May medal by a stroke, Arthur would be one ahead in the June competition, only to be nosed out again in July. It was a state of affairs which, had they been men of a more generous stamp, would have bred a mutual respect, esteem, and even love. But I am sorry to say that, apart from their golf, which was in a class of its own as far as this neighbourhood was concerned, Ralph Bingham and Arthur Jukes were a sorry pair – and yet, mark you, far from lacking in mere superficial good looks. They were handsome fellows, both of them, and well aware of the fact; and when Amanda Trivett came to stay they simply straightened their ties, twirled their moustaches, and expected her to do the rest.

But there they were disappointed. Perfectly friendly though she was to both of them, the love-light was conspicuously absent from her beautiful eyes. And it was not long before each had come independently to a solution of this mystery. It was plain to them that the whole trouble lay in the fact that each neutralized the other's attractions. Arthur felt that, if he could only have a clear field, all would be over except the sending out of the wedding invitations; and Ralph was of the opinion that, if he could just call on the girl one evening without finding the place all littered up with Arthur, his natural charms would swiftly bring home the bacon. And, indeed, it was true that they had no rivals except themselves. It happened at the moment that Woodhaven was very short of eligible bachelors. We marry young in this delightful spot, and all the likely men were already paired off. It seemed that, if Amanda Trivett intended to get married, she would have to select either Ralph Bingham or Arthur Jukes. A dreadful choice.

* * * * * * * * *

It had not occurred to me at the outset that my position in the affair would be anything closer than that of a detached and mildly interested spectator. Yet it was to me that Ralph came in his hour of need. When I returned home one evening, I found that my man had brought him in and laid him on the mat in my sitting-room.

I offered him a chair and a cigar, and he came to the point with commendable rapidity.

'Leigh,' he said, directly he had lighted his cigar, 'is too small for Arthur Jukes and myself.'

'Ah, you have been talking it over and decided to move?' I said, delighted. 'I think you are perfectly right. Leigh *is* over-built. Men like you and Jukes need a lot of space. Where do you think of going?'

'I'm not going?'

'But I thought you said—'

'What I meant was that the time has come when one of us must leave.'

'Oh, only one of you?' It was something, of course, but I confess I was disappointed, and I think my disappointment must have shown in my voice; for he looked at me, surprised.

'Surely you wouldn't mind Jukes going?' he said.

'Why, certainly not. He really is going, is he?'

A look of saturnine determination came into Ralph's face.

'He is. He thinks he isn't, but he is.'

I failed to understand him, and said so. He looked cautiously about the room, as if to reassure himself that he could not be overheard.

'I suppose you've noticed,' he said, 'the disgusting way that man Jukes has been hanging round Miss Trivett, boring her to death?'

'I have seen them together sometimes.'

'I love Amanda Trivett!' said Ralph.

'Poor girl!' I sighed.

'I beg your pardon?'

'Poor girl!' I said. 'I mean, to have Arthur Jukes hanging round her.'

'That's just what I think,' said Ralph Bingham. 'And that's why we're going to play this match.'

'What match?'

'This match we've decided to play. I want you to act as one of the judges, to go along with Jukes and see that he doesn't play any of his tricks. You know what he is! And in a vital match like this—'

'How much are you playing for?'

'The whole world!'

'I beg your pardon?'

'The whole world. It amounts to that. The loser is to leave Leigh for good, and the winner stays on and marries Amanda Trivett. We have arranged all the details. Rupert Bailey will accompany me, acting as the other judge.'

'And you want me to go round with Jukes?'

'Not round,' said Ralph Bingham. 'Along.'

'What is the distinction?'

'We are not going to play a round. Only one hole.'

'Sudden death, eh?'

'Not so very sudden. It's a longish hole. We start on the first tee here and hole out in the town in the doorway of the Majestic Hotel in Royal Square. A distance, I imagine, of about sixteen miles.'

I was revolted. About that time a perfect epidemic of freak matches had broken out in the club, and I had strongly opposed them from the start. George Willis had begun it by playing a medal round with the pro., George's first nine against the pro.'s complete eighteen. After that came the contest between Herbert Widgeon and Montague Brown, the latter, a twenty-four handicap man, being entitled to shout 'Boo!' three times during the round at moments selected by himself. There had been many more of these degrading travesties on the sacred game, and I had writhed to see them. Playing freak golf-matches is to my mind like ragging a great classical melody. But of the whole collection this one, considering the sentimental interest and the magnitude of the stakes, seemed to me the most terrible. My face, I imagine, betrayed my disgust, for Bingham attempted extenuation.

'It's the only way,' he said. 'You know how Jukes and I are on the links. We are as level as two men can be. This, of course, is due to his extraordinary luck. Everybody knows that he is the world's champion fluker. I, on the other hand, invariably have the worst luck. The consequence is that in an ordinary round it is always a toss-up which of us wins. The test we propose will eliminate luck. After sixteen miles of give-and-take play, I am certain – that is to say, the better man is certain to be ahead. That is what I meant when I said that Arthur Jukes would shortly be leaving Leigh. Well, may I take it that you will consent to act as one of the judges?'

I considered. After all, the match was likely to be historic, and one always feels tempted to hand one's name down to posterity.

'Very well,' I said.

'Excellent. You will have to keep a sharp eye on Jukes, I need scarcely remind you. You will, of course, carry a book of the rules in your pocket and refer to them when you wish to refresh your memory. We start at daybreak, for, if we put it off till later, the course at the other end might be somewhat congested when we reached it. We want to avoid publicity as far as possible. If I took a full iron and hit a policeman, it would excite remark.'

'It would. I can tell you the exact remark which it would excite.'

'We shall take bicycles with us, to minimize the fatigue of covering the distance. Well, I am glad that we have your co-operation. At daybreak to-morrow on the first tee, and don't forget to bring your rule-book.'

* * * * * * * * *

The atmosphere brooding over the first tee, when I reached it on the following morning, somewhat resembled that of a duelling-ground in the days when these affairs were settled with rapiers or pistols. Rupert Bailey, an old friend of mine, was the only cheerful member of the party. I am never at my best in the early morning, and the two rivals glared at each other with silent sneers. I had never supposed till that moment that men ever really sneered at one another outside the movies, but these two were indisputably doing so. They were in the mood when men say 'Pshaw!'

They tossed for the honour, and Arthur Jukes, having won, drove off with a fine ball that landed well down the course. Ralph Bingham, having teed up, turned to Rupert Bailey.

'Go down on to the fairway of the seventeenth,' he said. 'I want you to mark my ball.'

Rupert stared.

'The seventeenth!'

'I am going to take that direction,' said Ralph, pointing over the trees.

'But that will land your second or third shot in the lake.'

'I have provided for that. I have a flat-bottomed boat moored close by the sixteenth green. I shall use a mashie-niblick and chip my ball aboard, row across to the other side, chip it ashore, and carry on. I propose to go across country as far as Woodfield. I think it will save me a stroke or two.'

I gasped. I had never before realized the man's devilish cunning. His tactics gave him a flying start. Arthur, who had driven straight down the course, had as his objective the high road, which adjoins the waste ground beyond the first green. Once there, he would play the orthodox game by driving his ball along till he reached the bridge. While Arthur was winding along the high road, Ralph would have cut off practically two sides of a triangle. And it was hopeless for Arthur to imitate his enemy's tactics now. From where his ball lay he would have to cross a wide tract of marsh in order to reach the seventeenth fairway – an impossible feat. And, even if it had been feasible, he had no boat to take him across the water.

He uttered a violent protest. He was an unpleasant young man, almost – it seems absurd to say so, but almost as unpleasant as Ralph Bingham; yet at the moment I am bound to say I sympathized with him.

'What are you doing?' he demanded. 'You can't play fast and loose with the rules like that.'

'To what rule do you refer?' said Ralph, coldly.

'Well, that bally boat of yours is a hazard, isn't it? And you can't row a hazard about all over the place.'

'Why not?'

The simple question seemed to take Arthur Jukes aback.

'Why not?' he repeated. 'Why not? Well, you can't. That's why.'

'There is nothing in the rules,' said Ralph Bingham, 'against moving a hazard. If a hazard can be moved without disturbing the ball, you are at liberty, I gather, to move it wherever you please. Besides, what is all this about moving hazards? I have a perfect right to go for a morning row, haven't I? If I were to ask my doctor, he would probably actually recommend it. I am going to row my boat across the sound. If it happens to have my ball on board, that is not my affair. I shall not disturb my ball, and I shall play it from where it lies. Am I right in saying that the rules enact that the ball shall be played from where it lies?'

We admitted that it was.

'Very well, then,' said Ralph Bingham. 'Don't let us waste any more time. We will wait for you at Woodfield.'

He addressed his ball, and drove a beauty over the trees. It flashed out of sight in the direction of the seventeenth tee. Arthur and I made our way down the hill to play our second.

* * * * * * * * *

It is a curious trait of the human mind that, however little personal interest one may have in the result, it is impossible to prevent oneself taking sides in any event of a competitive nature. I had embarked on this affair in a purely neutral spirit, not caring which of the two won and only sorry that both could not lose. Yet, as the morning wore on, I found myself almost unconsciously becoming distinctly pro-Jukes. I did not like the man. I objected to his face, his manners, and the colour of his tie. Yet there was something in the dogged way in which he struggled against adversity which touched me and won my grudging support. Many men, I felt, having been so outmanœuvred at the start, would have given up the contest in despair; but Arthur Jukes, for all his defects, had the soul of a true golfer. He declined to give up. In grim silence he hacked his ball through the rough till he reached the high road; and then, having played twenty-seven, set himself resolutely to propel it on its long journey.

It was a lovely morning, and, as I bicycled along, keeping a fatherly eye on Arthur's activities, I realized for the first time in my life the full meaning of that exquisite phrase of Coleridge: –

Clothing the palpable and familiar
With golden exhalations of the dawn,

for in the pellucid air everything seemed weirdly beautiful, even Arthur Jukes's heather-mixture knickerbockers, of which hitherto I had never approved. The sun gleamed on their seat, as he bent to make his shots, in a cheerful and almost a poetic way. The birds were singing gaily in the hedgerows, and such was my uplifted state that I, too, burst into song, until Arthur petulantly desired me to refrain, on the plea that, though he yielded to no man in his enjoyment of farmyard imitations in their proper place, I put him off his stroke. And so we passed through Bayside in silence and started to cover that long stretch of road which ends in the railway bridge and the gentle descent into Woodfield.

Arthur was not doing badly. He was at least keeping them straight. And in the circumstances straightness was to be preferred to distance. Soon after leaving Little Hadley he had become ambitious and had used his brassey with disastrous results, slicing his fifty-third into the rough on the right of the road. It had taken him ten with the niblick to get back on to the car tracks, and this had taught him prudence.

He was now using his putter for every shot, and, except when he got trapped in the cross-lines at the top of the hill just before reaching Bayside, he had been in no serious difficulties. He was playing a nice easy game, getting the full face of the putter on to each shot.

At the top of the slope that drops down into Woodfield High Street he paused.

'I think I might try my brassey again here,' he said. 'I have a nice lie.'

'Is it wise?' I said.

He looked down the hill.

'What I was thinking,' he said, 'was that with it I might wing that man Bingham. I see he is standing right out in the middle of the fairway.'

I followed his gaze. It was perfectly true. Ralph Bingham was leaning on his bicycle in the roadway, smoking a cigarette. Even at this distance one could detect the man's disgustingly complacent expression. Rupert Bailey was sitting with his back against the door of the Woodfield Garage, looking rather used up. He was a man who liked to keep himself clean and tidy, and it was plain that the cross-country trip had done him no good. He seemed to be scraping mud off his face. I learned later that he had had the misfortune to fall into a ditch just beyond Bayside.

'No,' said Arthur. 'On second thoughts, the safe game is the one to play. I'll stick to the putter.'

We dropped down the hill, and presently came up with the opposition. I had not been mistaken in thinking that Ralph Bingham looked complacent. The man was smirking.

'Playing three hundred and ninety-six,' he said, as we drew near. 'How are you?'

I consulted my score-card.

'We have played a snappy seven hundred and eleven,' I said.

Ralph exulted openly. Rupert Bailey made no comment. He was too busy with the alluvial deposits on his person.

'Perhaps you would like to give up the match?' said Ralph to Arthur.

'Tchah!' said Arthur.

'Might just as well.'

'Pah!' said Arthur.

'You can't win now.'

'Pshaw!' said Arthur.

I am aware that Arthur's dialogue might have been brighter, but he had been through a trying time.

Rupert Bailey sidled up to me.

'I'm going home,' he said.

'Nonsense!' I replied. 'You are in an official capacity. You must stick to your post. Besides, what could be nicer than a pleasant morning ramble?'

'Pleasant morning ramble my number nine foot!' he replied, peevishly. 'I want to get back to civilization and set an excavating party with pickaxes to work on me.'

'You take too gloomy a view of the matter. You are a little dusty. Nothing more.'

'And it's not only the being buried alive that I mind. I cannot stick Ralph Bingham much longer.'

'You have found him trying?'

'Trying! Why, after I had fallen into that ditch and was coming up for the third time, all the man did was simply to call to me to admire an infernal iron shot he had just made. No sympathy, mind you! Wrapped up in himself. Why don't you make your man give up the match? He can't win.'

'I refuse to admit it. Much may happen between here and Royal Square.'

I have seldom known a prophecy more swiftly fulfilled. At this moment the doors of the Woodfield Garage opened and a small car rolled out with a grimy young man in a sweater at the wheel. He brought the machine out into the road, and alighted and went back into the garage, where we heard him shouting unintelligibly to someone in the rear premises. The car remained puffing and panting against the kerb.

Engaged in conversation with Rupert Bailey, I was paying little attention to this evidence of an awakening world, when suddenly I heard a hoarse, triumphant cry from Arthur Jukes, and, turning, I perceived his ball dropping neatly into the car's interior. Arthur himself, brandishing a niblick, was dancing about in the fairway.

'Now what about your moving hazards?' he cried.

At this moment the man in the sweater returned, carrying a spanner. Arthur Jukes sprang towards him.

'I'll give you five pounds to drive me to Royal Square,' he said.

I do not know what the sweater-clad young man's engagements for the morning had been originally, but nothing could have been more obliging than the ready way in which he consented to revise them at a moment's notice. I dare say you have noticed that the sturdy peasantry of our beloved land respond to an offer of five pounds as to a bugle-call.

'You're on,' said the youth.

'Good!' said Arthur Jukes.

'You think you're darned clever,' said Ralph Bingham.

'I know it,' said Arthur.

'Well, then,' said Ralph, 'perhaps you will tell us how you propose to get the ball out of the car when you reach Royal Square?'

'Certainly,' replied Arthur. 'You will observe on the side of the vehicle a convenient handle which, when turned, opens the door. The door thus opened, I shall chip my ball out!'

'I see,' said Ralph. 'Yes, I never thought of that.'

There was something in the way the man spoke that I did not like. His mildness seemed to me suspicious. He had the air of a man who has something up his sleeve. I was still musing on this when Arthur called to me impatiently to get in. I did so, and we drove off. Arthur was in great spirits. He had ascertained from the young man at the wheel that there was no chance of the opposition being able to hire another car at the garage. This machine was his own property, and the only other one at present in the shop was suffering from complicated trouble of the oiling-system and would not be able to be moved for at least another day.

I, however, shook my head when he pointed out the advantages of his position. I was still wondering about Ralph.

'I don't like it,' I said.

'Don't like what?'

'Ralph Bingham's manner.'

'Of course not,' said Arthur. 'Nobody does. There have been complaints on all sides.'

'I mean, when you told him how you intended to get the ball out of the car.'

'What was the matter with him?'

'He was too – ha!'

'How do you mean he was too – ha?'

'I have it!'

'What?'

'I see the trap he was laying for you. It has just dawned on me. No wonder he didn't object to your opening the door and chipping the ball out. By doing so you would forfeit the match.'

'Nonsense! Why?'

'Because,' I said, 'it is against the rules to tamper with a hazard. If you had got into a sand-bunker, would you smooth away the sand? If you had put your shot under a tree, could your caddie hold up the branches to give you a clear shot? Obviously you would disqualify yourself if you touched that door.'

Arthur's jaw dropped.

'What! Then how the deuce am I to get it out?'

'That,' I said, gravely, 'is a question between you and your Maker.'

It was here that Arthur Jukes forfeited the sympathy which I had begun to feel for him. A crafty, sinister look came into his eyes.

'Listen!' he said. 'It'll take them an hour to catch up with us. Suppose, during that time, that door happened to open accidentally, as it were, and close again? You wouldn't think it necessary to mention the fact, eh? You would be a good fellow and keep your mouth shut, yes? You might even see your way to go so far as to back me up in a statement to the effect that I hooked it out with my—?'

I was revolted.

'I am a golfer,' I said, coldly, 'and I obey the rules.'

'Yes, but—'

'Those rules were drawn up by—' – I bared my head reverently – 'by the Committee of the Royal and Ancient at St Andrews. I have always respected them, and I shall not deviate on this occasion from the policy of a lifetime.'

Arthur Jukes relapsed into a moody silence. He broke it once, crossing the West Street Bridge, to observe that he would like to know if I called myself a friend of his – a question which I was able to answer with a whole-hearted negative. After that he did not speak till the car drew up in front of the Majestic Hotel in Royal Square.

Early as the hour was, a certain bustle and animation already prevailed in that centre of the city, and the spectacle of a man in a golf-coat and plus-four knickerbockers hacking with a niblick at the floor of a car was not long in collecting a crowd of some dimensions. Three messenger-boys, four typists, and a gentleman in full evening dress, who obviously possessed or was friendly with someone who possessed a large cellar, formed the nucleus of it; and they were joined about the time when Arthur addressed the ball in order to play his nine hundred and fifteenth by six news-boys, eleven charladies, and perhaps a dozen assorted loafers, all speculating with the liveliest interest as to which particular asylum had had the honour of sheltering Arthur before he had contrived to elude the vigilance of his custodians.

Arthur had prepared for some such contingency. He suspended his activities with the niblick, and drew from his pocket a large poster, which he proceeded to hang over the side of the car. It read: –

COME

TO

McCLURG AND MACDONALD,

18, WEST STREET,

FOR

ALL GOLFING SUPPLIES.

His knowledge of psychology had not misled him. Directly they gathered that he was advertising something, the crowd declined to look at it; they melted away, and Arthur returned to his work in solitude.

He was taking a well-earned rest after playing his eleven hundred and fifth, a nice niblick shot with lots of wrist behind it, when out of Bridle Street there trickled a weary-looking golf-ball, followed in the order named by Ralph Bingham, resolute but going a trifle at the knees, and Rupert Bailey on a bicycle. The latter, on whose face and limbs the mud had dried, made an arresting spectacle.

'What are you playing?' I inquired.

'Eleven hundred,' said Rupert. 'We got into a casual dog.'

'A casual dog?'

'Yes, just before the bridge. We were coming along nicely, when a stray dog grabbed our nine hundred and ninety-eighth and took it nearly back to Woodfield, and we had to start all over again. How are you getting on?'

'We have just played our eleven hundred and fifth. A nice even game.' I looked at Ralph's ball, which was lying close to the kerb. 'You are farther from the hole, I think. Your shot, Bingham.'

Rupert Bailey suggested breakfast. He was a man who was altogether too fond of creature comforts. He had not the true golfing spirit.

'Breakfast!' I exclaimed.

'Breakfast,' said Rupert, firmly. 'If you don't know what it is, I can teach you in half a minute. You play it with a pot of coffee, a knife and fork, and about a hundred-weight of scrambled eggs. Try it. It's a pastime that grows on you.'

I was surprised when Ralph Bingham supported the suggestion. He was so near holing out that I should have supposed that nothing would have kept him from finishing the match. But he agreed heartily.

'Breakfast,' he said, 'is an excellent idea. You go along in. I'll follow in a moment. I want to buy a paper.'

We went into the hotel, and a few minutes later he joined us. Now that we were actually at the table, I confess that the idea of breakfast was by no means repugnant to me. The keen air and the exercise had given me an appetite, and it was some little time before I was able to assure the waiter definitely that he could cease bringing orders of scrambled eggs. The others having finished also, I suggested a move. I was anxious to get the match over and be free to go home.

We filed out of the hotel, Arthur Jukes leading. When I had passed through the swing-doors, I found him gazing perplexedly up and down the street.

'What is the matter?' I asked.

'It's gone!'

'What has gone?'

'The car!'

'Oh, the car?' said Ralph Bingham. 'That's all right. Didn't I tell you about that? I bought it just now and engaged the driver as my chauffeur. I've been meaning to buy a car for a long time. A man ought to have a car.'

'Where is it?' said Arthur, blankly. The man seemed dazed.

'I couldn't tell you to a mile or two,' replied Ralph. 'I told the man to drive to Glasgow. Why? Had you any message for him?'

'But my ball was inside it!'

'Now that,' said Ralph, 'is really unfortunate! Do you mean to tell me you hadn't managed to get it out yet? Yes, that *is* a little awkward for you. I'm afraid it means that you lose the match.'

'Lose the match?'

'Certainly. The rules are perfectly definite on that point. A period of five minutes is allowed for each stroke. The player who fails to make his stroke within that time loses the hole. Unfortunate, but there it is!'

Arthur Jukes sank down on the path and buried his face in his hands. He had the appearance of a broken man. Once more, I am bound to say, I felt a certain pity for him. He had certainly struggled gamely, and it was hard to be beaten like this on the post.

'Playing eleven hundred and one,' said Ralph Bingham, in his odiously self-satisfied voice, as he addressed his ball. He laughed jovially. A messenger-boy had paused close by and was watching the proceedings gravely. Ralph Bingham patted him on the head.

'Well, sonny,' he said, 'what club would *you* use here?'

'I claim the match!' cried Arthur Jukes, springing up. Ralph Bingham regarded him coldly.

'I beg your pardon?'

'I claim the match!' repeated Arthur Jukes. 'The rules say that a player who asks advice from any person other than his caddie shall lose the hole.'

'This is absurd!' said Ralph, but I noticed that he had turned pale.

'I appeal to the judges.'

'We sustain the appeal,' I said, after a brief consultation with Rupert Bailey. 'The rule is perfectly clear.'

'But you had lost the match already by not playing within five minutes,' said Ralph, vehemently.

'It was not my turn to play. You were farther from the pin.'

'Well, play now. Go on! Let's see you make your shot.'

'There is no necessity,' said Arthur, frigidly. 'Why should I play when you have already disqualified yourself?'

'I claim a draw!'

'I deny the claim.'

'I appeal to the judges.'

'Very well. We will leave it to the judges.'

I consulted with Rupert Bailey. It seemed to me that Arthur Jukes was entitled to the verdict. Rupert, who, though an amiable and delightful companion, had always been one of Nature's fat-heads, could not see it. We had to go back to our principals and announce that we had been unable to agree.

'This is ridiculous,' said Ralph Bingham. 'We ought to have had a third judge.'

At this moment, who should come out of the hotel but Amanda Trivett! A veritable goddess from the machine.

'It seems to me,' I said, 'that you would both be well advised to leave the decision to Miss Trivett. You could have no better referee.'

'I'm game,' said Arthur Jukes.

'Suits *me*,' said Ralph Bingham.

'Why, whatever are you all doing here with your golf-clubs?' asked the girl, wonderingly.

'These two gentlemen,' I explained, 'have been playing a match, and a point has arisen on which the judges do not find themselves in agreement. We need an unbiased outside opinion, and we should like to put it up to you. The facts are as follows: –'

Amanda Trivett listened attentively, but, when I had finished, she shook her head.

'I'm afraid I don't know enough about the game to be able to decide a question like that,' she said.

'Then we must consult St Andrews,' said Rupert Bailey.

'I'll tell you who might know,' said Amanda Trivett, after a moment's thought.

'Who is that?' I asked.

'My *fiancé*. He has just come back from a golfing holiday. That's why I'm in town this morning. I've been to meet him. He is very good at golf. He won a medal at Little-Mudbury-in-the-Wold the day before he left.'

There was a tense silence. I had the delicacy not to look at Ralph or Arthur. Then the silence was broken by a sharp crack. Ralph Bingham had broken his mashie-niblick across his knee. From the direction where Arthur Jukes was standing there came a muffled gulp.

'Shall I ask him?' said Amanda Trivett.

'Don't bother,' said Ralph Bingham.

'It doesn't matter,' said Arthur Jukes.

8 THE HEEL OF ACHILLES

On the young man's face, as he sat sipping his ginger-ale in the club-house smoking-room, there was a look of disillusionment. 'Never again!' he said.

The Oldest Member glanced up from his paper.

'You are proposing to give up golf once more?' he queried.

'Not golf. Betting on golf.' The Young Man frowned. 'I've just been let down badly. Wouldn't you have thought I had a good thing, laying seven to one on McTavish against Robinson?'

'Undoubtedly,' said the Sage. 'The odds, indeed, generous as they are, scarcely indicate the former's superiority. Do you mean to tell me that the thing came unstitched?'

'Robinson won in a walk, after being three down at the turn.'

'Strange! What happened?'

'Why, they looked in at the bar to have a refresher before starting for the tenth,' said the young man, his voice quivering, 'and McTavish suddenly discovered that there was a hole in his trouser-pocket and sixpence had dropped out. He worried so frightfully about it that on the second nine he couldn't do a thing right. Went completely off his game and didn't win a hole.'

The Sage shook his head gravely.

'If this is really going to be a lesson to you, my boy, never to bet on the result of a golf-match, it will be a blessing in disguise.

There is no such thing as a certainty in golf. I wonder if I ever told you a rather curious episode in the career of Vincent Jopp?'

'*The* Vincent Jopp? The American multi-millionaire?'

'The same. You never knew he once came within an ace of winning the American Amateur Championship, did you?'

'I never heard of his playing golf.'

'He played for one season. After that he gave it up and has not touched a club since. Ring the bell and get me a small lime-juice, and I will tell you all.'

* * * * * * * * *

It was long before your time (said the Oldest Member) that the events which I am about to relate took place. I had just come down from Cambridge, and was feeling particularly pleased with myself because I had secured the job of private and confidential secretary to Vincent Jopp, then a man in the early thirties, busy in laying the foundations of his present remarkable fortune. He engaged me, and took me with him to Chicago.

Jopp was, I think, the most extraordinary personality I have encountered in a long and many-sided life. He was admirably equipped for success in finance, having the steely eye and square jaw without which it is hopeless for a man to enter that line of business. He possessed also an overwhelming confidence in himself, and the ability to switch a cigar from one corner of his mouth to the other without wiggling his ears, which, as you know, is the stamp of the true Monarch of the Money Market. He was the nearest approach to the financier on the films, the fellow who makes his jaw-muscles jump when he is telephoning, that I have ever seen.

Like all successful men, he was a man of method. He kept a pad on his desk on which he would scribble down his appointments, and it was my duty on entering the office each morning to take this pad and type its contents neatly in a loose-leaved ledger. Usually, of course, these entries referred to business appointments and deals which he was contemplating, but one day I was interested to note, against the date May 3rd, the entry: –

Propose to Amelia.

I was interested, as I say, but not surprised. Though a man of steel and iron, there was nothing of the celibate about Vincent Jopp. He was one of those men who marry early and often. On three separate occasions before I joined his service he had jumped off the dock, to scramble back to shore again later by means of the Divorce Court lifebelt. Scattered here and there about the country there were three ex-Mrs Jopps, drawing their monthly envelope, and now, it seemed, he contemplated the addition of a fourth to the platoon.

I was not surprised, I say, at this resolve of his. What did seem a little remarkable to me was the thorough way in which he had thought the thing out. This iron-willed man recked nothing of possible obstacles. Under the date of June 1st was the entry: –

Marry Amelia;

while in March of the following year he had arranged to have his first-born christened Thomas Reginald. Later on, the short-coating of Thomas Reginald was arranged for, and there was a note about sending him to school. Many hard things have been said of Vincent Jopp, but nobody has ever accused him of not being a man who looked ahead.

On the morning of May 4th Jopp came into the office, looking, I fancied, a little thoughtful. He sat for some moments staring before him with his brow a trifle furrowed; then he seemed to come to himself. He rapped his desk.

'Hi! You!' he said. It was thus that he habitually addressed me.

'Mr Jopp?' I replied.

'What's golf?'

I had at that time just succeeded in getting my handicap down into single figures, and I welcomed the opportunity of dilating on the noblest of pastimes. But I had barely begun my eulogy when he stopped me.

'It's a game, is it?'

'I suppose you could call it that,' I said, 'but it is an off-hand way of describing the holiest—'

'How do you play it?'

'Pretty well,' I said. 'At the beginning of the season I didn't seem able to keep 'em straight at all, but lately I've been doing fine. Getting better every day. Whether it was that I was moving my head or gripping too tightly with the right hand—'

'Keep the reminiscences for your grandchildren during the long winter evenings,' he interrupted, abruptly, as was his habit. 'What I want to know is what a fellow does when he plays golf. Tell me in as few words as you can just what it's all about.'

'You hit a ball with a stick till it falls into a hole.'

'Easy!' he snapped. 'Take dictation.'

I produced my pad.

'May the fifth, take up golf. What's an Amateur Championship?'

'It is the annual competition to decide which is the best player among the amateurs. There is also a Professional Championship, and an Open event.'

'Oh, there are golf professionals, are there? What do they do?'

'They teach golf.'

'Which is the best of them?'

'Sandy McHoots won both British and American Open events last year.'

'Wire him to come here at once.'

'But McHoots is in Inverlochty, in Scotland.'

'Never mind. Get him; tell him to name his own terms. When is the Amateur Championship?'

'I think it is on September the twelfth this year.'

'All right, take dictation. September twelfth, win Amateur Championship.'

I stared at him in amazement, but he was not looking at me.

'Got that?' he said. 'September thir— Oh, I was forgetting! Add September twelfth, corner wheat. September thirteenth, marry Amelia.'

'Marry Amelia,' I echoed, moistening my pencil.

'Where do you play this – what's-its-name – golf?'

'There are clubs all over the country. I belong to the Wissahicky Glen.'

'That a good place?'

'Very good.'

'Arrange to-day for my becoming a member.'

* * * * * * * * *

Sandy McHoots arrived in due course, and was shown into the private office.

'Mr McHoots?' said Vincent Jopp.

'Mphm!' said the Open Champion.

'I have sent for you, Mr McHoots, because I hear that you are the greatest living exponent of this game of golf.'

'Aye,' said the champion, cordially. 'I am that.'

'I wish you to teach me the game. I am already somewhat behind schedule owing to the delay incident upon your long journey, so let us start at once. Name a few of the most important points in connection with the game. My secretary will make notes of them, and I will memorize them. In this way we shall save time. Now, what is the most important thing to remember when playing golf?'

'Keep your heid still.'

'A simple task.'

'Na sae simple as it soonds.'

'Nonsense!' said Vincent Jopp, curtly. 'If I decide to keep my head still, I shall keep it still. What next?'

'Keep yer ee on the ba'.'

'It shall be attended to. And the next?'

'Dinna press.'

'I won't. And to resume.'

Mr McHoots ran through a dozen of the basic rules, and I took them down in shorthand. Vincent Jopp studied the list.

'Very good. Easier than I had supposed. On the first tee at Wissahicky Glen at eleven sharp to-morrow, Mr McHoots. Hi! You!'

'Sir?' I said.

'Go out and buy me a set of clubs, a red jacket, a cloth cap, a pair of spiked shoes, and a ball.'

'One ball?'

'Certainly. What need is there of more?'

'It sometimes happens,' I explained, 'that a player who is learning the game fails to hit his ball straight, and then he often loses it in the rough at the side of the fairway.'

'Absurd!' said Vincent Jopp. 'If I set out to drive my ball straight, I shall drive it straight. Good morning, Mr McHoots. You will excuse me now. I am busy cornering Woven Textiles.'

* * * * * * * * *

Golf is in its essence a simple game. You laugh in a sharp, bitter, barking manner when I say this, but nevertheless it is true. Where the average man goes wrong is in making the game difficult for himself. Observe the non-player, the man who walks round with you for the sake of the fresh air. He will hole out with a single care-free flick of his umbrella the twenty-foot putt over which you would ponder and hesitate for a full minute before sending it right off the line. Put a driver in his hands, and he pastes the ball into the next county without a thought. It is only when he takes to the game in earnest that he becomes self-conscious and anxious, and tops his shots even as you and I. A man who could retain through his golfing career the almost scornful confidence of the non-player would be unbeatable. Fortunately such an attitude of mind is beyond the scope of human nature.

It was not, however, beyond the scope of Vincent Jopp, the superman. Vincent Jopp was, I am inclined to think, the only golfer who ever approached the game in a spirit of Pure Reason. I have read of men who, never having swum in their lives, studied a text-book on their way down to the swimming bath, mastered its contents, and dived in and won the big race. In just such a spirit did Vincent Jopp start to play golf. He committed McHoots's hints to memory, and then went out on the links and put them into practice. He came to the tee with a clear picture in his mind of what he had to do, and he did it. He was not intimidated, like the average novice, by the thought that if he pulled in his hands he would slice, or if he gripped too tightly with the right he would pull. Pulling in the hands was an error, so he did not pull in his hands. Gripping too tightly was a defect, so he did not grip too tightly. With that weird concentration which had served him so well in business he did precisely what he had set out to do – no less and no more. Golf with Vincent Jopp was an exact science.

The annals of the game are studded with the names of those who have made rapid progress in their first season. Colonel Quill, we read in our Vardon, took up golf at the age of fifty-six, and by devising an ingenious machine consisting of a fishing-line and a sawn-down bedpost was enabled to keep his head so still that he became a scratch player before the end of the year. But no one, I imagine, except Vincent Jopp, has ever achieved scratch on his first morning on the links.

The main difference, we are told, between the amateur and the professional golfer is the fact that the latter is always aiming at the pin, while the former has in his mind a vague picture of getting somewhere reasonably near it. Vincent Jopp invariably went for the pin. He tried to hole out from anywhere inside two hundred and twenty yards. The only occasion on which I ever heard him express any chagrin or disappointment was during the afternoon round on his first day out, when from the tee on the two-hundred-and-eighty-yard seventh he laid his ball within six inches of the hole.

'A marvellous shot!' I cried, genuinely stirred.

'Too much to the right,' said Vincent Jopp, frowning.

He went on from triumph to triumph. He won the monthly medal in May, June, July, August, and September. Towards the end of May he was heard to complain that Wissahicky Glen was not a sporting course. The Greens Committee sat up night after night trying to adjust his handicap so as to give other members an outside chance against him. The golf experts of the daily papers wrote columns about his play. And it was pretty generally considered throughout the country that it would be a pure formality for anyone else to enter against him in the Amateur

Championship – an opinion which was borne out when he got through into the final without losing a hole. A safe man to have betted on, you would have said. But mark the sequel.

* * * * * * * * *

The American Amateur Championship was held that year in Detroit. I had accompanied my employer there; for, though engaged on this nerve-wearing contest, he refused to allow his business to be interfered with. As he had indicated in his schedule, he was busy at the time cornering wheat; and it was my task to combine the duties of caddie and secretary. Each day I accompanied him round the links with my note-book and his bag of clubs, and the progress of his various matches was somewhat complicated by the arrival of a stream of telegraph-boys bearing important messages. He would read these between the strokes and dictate replies to me, never, however, taking more than the five minutes allowed by the rules for an interval between strokes. I am inclined to think that it was this that put the finishing touch on his opponents' discomfiture. It is not soothing for a nervous man to have the game hung up on the green while his adversary dictates to his caddie a letter beginning 'Yours of the 11th inst. received and contents noted. In reply would state—' This sort of thing puts a man off his game.

I was resting in the lobby of our hotel after a strenuous day's work, when I found that I was being paged. I answered the summons, and was informed that a lady wished to see me. Her card bore the name 'Miss Amelia Merridew.' Amelia! The name seemed familiar. Then I remembered. Amelia was the name of the girl Vincent Jopp intended to marry, the fourth of the long line of Mrs Jopps. I hurried to present myself, and found a tall, slim girl, who was plainly labouring under a considerable agitation.

'Miss Merridew?' I said.

'Yes,' she murmured. 'My name will be strange to you.'

'Am I right,' I queried, 'in supposing that you are the lady to whom Mr Jopp—'

'I am! I am!' she replied. 'And, oh, what shall I do?'

'Kindly give me particulars,' I said, taking out my pad from force of habit.

She hesitated a moment, as if afraid to speak.

'You are caddying for Mr Jopp in the Final to-morrow?' she said at last.

'I am.'

'Then could you – would you mind – would it be giving you too much trouble if I asked you to shout "Boo!" at him when he is making his stroke, if he looks like winning?'

I was perplexed.

'I don't understand.'

'I see that I must tell you all. I am sure you will treat what I say as absolutely confidential.'

'Certainly.'

'I am provisionally engaged to Mr Jopp.'

'Provisionally?'

She gulped.

'Let me tell you my story. Mr Jopp asked me to marry him, and I would rather do anything on earth than marry him. But how could I say "No!" with those awful eyes of his boring me through? I knew that if I said "No," he would argue me out of it in two minutes. I had an idea. I gathered that he had never played golf, so I told him that I would marry him if he won the Amateur Championship this year. And now I find that he has been a golfer all along, and, what is more, a plus man! It isn't fair!'

'He was not a golfer when you made that condition,' I said. 'He took up the game on the following day.'

'Impossible! How could he have become as good as he is in this short time?'

'Because he is Vincent Jopp! In his lexicon there is no such word as impossible.'

She shuddered.

'What a man! But I can't marry him,' she cried. 'I want to marry somebody else. Oh, won't you help me? Do shout "Boo!" at him when he is starting his down-swing!'

I shook my head.

'It would take more than a single "boo" to put Vincent Jopp off his stroke.'

'But won't you try it?'

'I cannot. My duty is to my employer.'

'Oh, do!'

'No, no. Duty is duty, and paramount with me. Besides, I have a bet on him to win.'

The stricken girl uttered a faint moan, and tottered away.

* * * * * * * * *

I was in our suite shortly after dinner that night, going over some of the notes I had made that day, when the telephone rang. Jopp was out at the time, taking a short stroll with his after-dinner cigar. I unhooked the receiver, and a female voice spoke.

'Is that Mr Jopp?'

'Mr Jopp's secretary speaking. Mr Jopp is out.'

'Oh, it's nothing important. Will you say that Mrs Luella Mainprice Jopp called up to wish him luck? I shall be on the course to-morrow to see him win the final.'

I returned to my notes. Soon afterwards the telephone rang again.

'Vincent, dear?'

'Mr Jopp's secretary speaking.'

'Oh, will you say that Mrs Jane Jukes Jopp called up to wish him luck? I shall be there to-morrow to see him play.'

I resumed my work. I had hardly started when the telephone rang for the thrid time.

'Mr Jopp?'

'Mr Jopp's secretary speaking.'

'This is Mrs Agnes Parsons Jopp. I just called up to wish him luck. I shall be looking on to-morrow.'

I shifted my work nearer to the telephone-table so as to be ready for the next call. I had heard that Vincent Jopp had only been married three times, but you never knew.

Presently Jopp came in.

'Anybody called up?' he asked.

'Nobody on business. An assortment of your wives were on the wire wishing you luck. They asked me to say that they will be on the course to-morrow.'

For a moment it seemed to me that the man's iron repose was shaken.

'Luella?' he asked.

'She was the first.'

'Jane?'

'And Jane.'

'And Agnes?'

'Agnes,' I said, 'is right.'

'H'm!' said Vincent Jopp. And for the first time since I had known him I thought that he was ill at ease.

* * * * * * * * *

The day of the final dawned bright and clear. At least, I was not awake at the time to see, but I suppose it did; for at nine o'clock, when I came down to breakfast, the sun was shining brightly. The first eighteen holes were to be played before lunch, starting at eleven. Until twenty minutes before the hour Vincent Jopp kept me busy taking dictation, partly on matters connected with his wheat deal and partly on a signed article dealing with the Final, entitled 'How I Won'. At eleven sharp we were out on the first tee.

Jopp's opponent was a nice-looking young man, but obviously nervous. He giggled in a distraught sort of way as he shook hands with my employer.

'Well, may the best man win,' he said.

'I have arranged to do so,' replied Jopp, curtly, and started to address his ball.

There was a large crowd at the tee, and, as Jopp started his down-swing, from somewhere on the outskirts of this crowd there came suddenly a musical 'Boo!' It rang out in the clear morning air like a bugle.

I had been right in my estimate of Vincent Jopp. His forceful stroke never wavered. The head of his club struck the ball, despatching it a good two hundred yards down the middle of the fairway. As we left the tee I saw Amelia Merridew being led away with bowed head by two members of the Greens Committee. Poor girl! My heart bled for her. And yet, after all, Fate had been kind in removing her from the scene, even in custody, for she could hardly have borne to watch the proceedings. Vincent Jopp made rings round his antagonist. Hole after hole he won in his remorseless, machine-like way, until when lunch-time came at the end of the eighteenth he was ten up. All the other holes had been halved.

It was after lunch, as we made our way to the first tee, that the advance-guard of the Mrs Jopps appeared in the person of

Luella Mainprice Jopp, a kittenish little woman with blonde hair and a Pekingese dog. I remembered reading in the papers that she had divorced my employer for persistent and aggravated mental cruelty, calling witnesses to bear out her statement that he had said he did not like her in pink, and that on two separate occasions had insisted on her dog eating the leg of a chicken instead of the breast; but Time, the great healer, seemed to have removed all bitterness, and she greeted him affectionately.

'Wassums going to win great big championship against nasty rough strong man?' she said.

'Such,' said Vincent Jopp, 'is my intention. It was kind of you, Luella, to trouble to come and watch me. I wonder if you know Mrs Agnes Parsons Jopp?' he said, courteously, indicating a kind-looking, motherly woman who had just come up. 'How are you, Agnes?'

'If you had asked me that question this morning, Vincent,' replied Mrs Agnes Parsons Jopp, 'I should have been obliged to say that I felt far from well. I had an odd throbbing feeling in the left elbow, and I am sure my temperature was above the normal. But this afternoon I am a little better. How are you, Vincent?'

Although she had, as I recalled from the reports of the case, been compelled some years earlier to request the Court to sever her marital relations with Vincent Jopp on the ground of calculated and inhuman brutality, in that he had callously refused, in spite of her pleadings, to take old Dr Bennett's Tonic Swamp-Juice three times a day, her voice, as she spoke, was kind and even anxious. Badly as this man had treated her – and I remember hearing that several of the jury had been unable to restrain their tears when she was in the witness-box giving her evidence – there still seemed to linger some remnants of the old affection.

'I am quite well, thank you, Agnes,' said Vincent Jopp.

'Are you wearing your liver-pad?'

A frown flitted across my employer's strong face.

'I am not wearing my liver-pad,' he replied, brusquely.

'Oh, Vincent, how rash of you!'

He was about to speak, when a sudden exclamation from his rear checked him. A genial-looking woman in a sports coat was standing there, eyeing him with a sort of humorous horror.

'Well, Jane,' he said.

I gathered that this was Mrs Jane Jukes Jopp, the wife who had divorced him for systematic and ingrowing fiendishness on the ground that he had repeatedly outraged her feelings by wearing a white waistcoat with a dinner-jacket. She continued to look at him dumbly, and then uttered a sort of strangled, hysterical laugh.

'Those legs!' she cried. 'Those legs!'

Vincent Jopp flushed darkly. Even the strongest and most silent of us have our weaknesses, and my employer's was the rooted idea that he looked well in knickerbockers. It was not my place to try to dissuade him, but there was no doubt that they did not suit him. Nature, in bestowing upon him a massive head and a jutting chin, had forgotten to finish him off at the other end. Vincent Jopp's legs were skinny.

'You poor dear man!' went on Mrs Jane Jukes Jopp. 'What practical joker ever lured you into appearing in public in knickerbockers?'

'I don't object to the knickerbockers,' said Mrs Agnes Parsons Jopp, 'but when he foolishly comes out in quite a strong east wind without his liver-pad—'

'Little Tinky-Ting don't need no liver-pad, he don't,' said Mrs Luella Mainprice Jopp, addressing the animal in her arms, 'because he was his muzzer's pet, he was.'

I was standing quite near to Vincent Jopp, and at this moment I saw a bead of perspiration spring out on his forehead, and into his steely eyes there came a positively hunted look. I could understand and sympathize. Napoleon himself would have wilted if he had found himself in the midst of a trio of females, one talking baby-talk, another fussing about his health, and the third making derogatory observations on his lower limbs. Vincent Jopp was becoming unstrung.

'May as well be starting, shall we?'

It was Jopp's opponent who spoke. There was a strange, set look on his face – the look of a man whose back is against the wall. Ten down on the morning's round, he had drawn on his reserves of courage and was determined to meet the inevitable bravely.

Vincent Jopp nodded absently, then turned to me.

'Keep those women away from me,' he whispered tensely. 'They'll put me off my stroke!'

'Put *you* off your stroke!' I exclaimed, incredulously.

'Yes, me! How the deuce can I concentrate, with people babbling about liver-pads, and – and knickerbockers all round me? Keep them away!'

He started to address his ball, and there was a weak uncertainty in the way he did it that prepared me for what was to come. His club rose, wavered, fell; and the ball, badly topped, trickled two feet and sank into a cuppy lie.

'Is that good or bad?' inquired Mrs Luella Mainprice Jopp.

A sort of desperate hope gleamed in the eye of the other competitor in the final. He swung with renewed vigour. His ball sang through the air, and lay within chip-shot distance of the green.

'At the very least,' said Mrs Agnes Parsons Jopp, 'I hope, Vincent, that you are wearing flannel next your skin.'

I heard Jopp give a stifled groan as he took his spoon from the bag. He made a gallant effort to retrieve the lost ground, but the ball struck a stone and bounded away into the long grass to the side of the green. His opponent won the hole.

We moved to the second tee.

'Now, *that* young man,' said Mrs Jane Jukes Jopp, indicating her late husband's blushing antagonist, 'is quite right to wear knickerbockers. He can carry them off. But a glance in the mirror must have shown you that you—'

'I'm sure you're feverish, Vincent,' said Mrs Agnes Parsons Jopp, solicitously. 'You are quite flushed. There is a wild gleam in your eyes.'

'Muzzer's pet's got little buttons of eyes, that don't never have no wild gleam in zem because he's muzzer's own darling, he was!' said Mrs Luella Mainprice Jopp.

A hollow groan escaped Vincent Jopp's ashen lips.

I need not recount the play hole by hole, I think. There are some subjects that are too painful. It was pitiful to watch Vincent Jopp in his downfall. By the end of the first nine his lead had been reduced to one, and his antagonist, rendered a new man by success, was playing magnificent golf. On the next hole he drew level. Then with a superhuman effort Jopp contrived to halve the eleventh, twelfth, and thirteenth. It seemed as though his iron will might still assert itself, but on the fourteenth the end came.

He had driven a superb ball, outdistancing his opponent by a full fifty yards. The latter played a good second to within a few feet of the green. And then, as Vincent Jopp was shaping for his stroke, Luella Mainprice gave tongue.

'Vincent!'

'Well?'

'Vincent, that other man – bad man – not playing fair. When your back was turned just now, he gave his ball a great bang. *I* was watching him.'

'At any rate,' said Mrs Agnes Parsons Jopp, 'I do hope, when the game is over, Vincent, that you will remember to cool slowly.'

'Flesho!' cried Mrs Jane Jukes Jopp triumphantly. 'I've been trying to remember the name all the afternoon. I saw about it in one of the papers. The advertisements speak most highly of it. You take it before breakfast and again before retiring, and they guarantee it to produce firm, healthy flesh on the most sparsely-covered limbs in next to no time. Now, *will* you remember to get a bottle to-night? It comes in two sizes, the five-shilling (or large size) and the smaller at half-a-crown. G. K. Chesterton writes that he used it regularly for years.'

Vincent Jopp uttered a quavering moan, and his hand, as he took the mashie from his bag, was trembling like an aspen.

Ten minutes later, he was on his way back to the club-house, a beaten man.

* * * * * * * * *

And so (concluded the Oldest Member) you see that in golf there is no such thing as a soft snap. You can never be certain of the finest player. Anything may happen to the greatest expert at any stage of the game. In a recent competition George Duncan took eleven shots over a hole which eighteen-handicap men generally do in five. No! Back horses or go down to Throgmorton Street and try to take it away from the Rothschilds, and I will applaud you as a shrewd and cautious financier. But to bet at golf is pure gambling.

9 THE ROUGH STUFF

Into the basking warmth of the day there had crept, with the approach of evening, that heartening crispness which heralds the advent of autumn. Already, in the valley by the ninth tee, some of the trees had begun to try on strange colours, in tentative experiment against the coming of nature's annual fancy dress ball, when the soberest tree casts off its workaday suit of green and plunges into a riot of reds and yellows. On the terrace in front of the club-house an occasional withered leaf fluttered down on the table where the Oldest Member sat, sipping a thoughtful seltzer and lemon and listening with courteous gravity to a young man in a sweater and golf breeches who occupied the neighbouring chair.

'She is a dear girl,' said the young man a little moodily, 'a dear girl in every respect. But somehow – I don't know – when I see her playing golf I can't help thinking that woman's place is in the home.'

The Oldest Member inclined his frosted head.

'You think,' he said, 'that lovely woman loses in queenly dignity when she fails to slam the ball squarely on the meat?'

'I don't mind her missing the pill,' said the young man. 'But I think her attitude toward the game is too light-hearted.'

'Perhaps it cloaks a deeper feeling. One of the noblest women I ever knew used to laugh merrily when she foozled a short putt. It was only later, when I learned that in the privacy of her home she would weep bitterly and bite holes in the sofa cushions, that I realized that she did but wear the mask. Continue to encourage your *fiancée* to play the game, my boy. Much happiness will reward you. I could tell you a story—'

A young woman of singular beauty and rather statuesque appearance came out of the club-house carrying a baby swaddled in flannel. As she drew near the table she said to the baby:

'Chicketty wicketty wicketty wipsey pop!'

In other respects her intelligence appeared to be above the ordinary.

'Isn't he a darling!' she said, addressing the Oldest Member.

The Sage cast a meditative eye upon the infant. Except to the eye of love, it looked like a skinned poached egg.

'Unquestionably so,' he replied.

'Don't you think he looks more like his father every day?'

For a brief instant the Oldest Member seemed to hesitate.

'Assuredly!' he said. 'Is your husband out on the links to-day?'

'Not to-day. He had to see Wilberforce off on the train to Scotland.'

'Your brother is going to Scotland?'

'Yes. Ramsden has such a high opinion of the schools up there. I did say that Scotland was a long way off, and he said yes, that had occurred to him, but that we must make sacrifices for Willie's good. He was very brave and cheerful about it. Well, I mustn't stay. There's quite a nip in the air, and Rammikins will get a nasty cold in his precious little button of a nose if I don't walk him about. Say "Bye-bye" to the gentlemen, Rammy!'

The Oldest Member watched her go thoughtfully.

'There is a nip in the air,' he said, 'and, unlike our late acquaintance in the flannel, I am not in my first youth. Come with me, I want to show you something.'

He led the way into the club-house, and paused before the wall of the smoking-room. This was decorated from top to bottom with bold caricatures of members of the club.

'These,' he said, 'are the work of a young newspaper artist who belongs here. A clever fellow. He has caught the expressions of these men wonderfully. His only failure, indeed, is that picture of myself.' He regarded it with distaste, and a touch of asperity crept into his manner. 'I don't know why the committee lets it stay there,' he said, irritably. 'It isn't a bit like.' He recovered himself. 'But all the others are excellent, excellent, though I believe many of the subjects are under the erroneous impression that they bear no resemblance to the originals. Here is the picture I wished to show you. That is Ramsden Waters, the husband of the lady who has just left us.'

The portrait which he indicated was that of a man in the early thirties. Pale saffron hair surmounted a receding forehead. Pale blue eyes looked out over a mouth which wore a pale, weak smile, from the centre of which protruded two teeth of a rabbit-like character.

'Golly! What a map!' exclaimed the young man at his side.

'Precisely!' said the Oldest Member. 'You now understand my momentary hesitation in agreeing with Mrs Waters that the baby was like its father. I was torn by conflicting emotions. On the one hand, politeness demanded that I confirm any statement made by a lady. Common humanity, on the other hand, made it repugnant to me to knock an innocent child. Yes, that is Ramsden Waters. Sit down and take the weight off your feet, and I will tell you about him. The story illustrates a favourite theory of mine, that it is an excellent thing that women should be encouraged to take up golf. There are, I admit, certain drawbacks attendant on their presence on the links. I shall not readily forget the occasion on which a low, raking drive of mine at the eleventh struck the ladies' tee box squarely and came back and stunned my caddie, causing me to lose stroke and distance. Nevertheless, I hold that the advantages outnumber the drawbacks. Golf humanizes women, humbles their haughty natures, tends, in short, to knock out of their systems a certain modicum of that superciliousness, that swank, which makes wooing a tough proposition for the diffident male. You may have found this yourself?'

'Well, as a matter of fact,' admitted the young man, 'now I come to think of it I have noticed that Genevieve has shown me a bit more respect since she took up the game. When I drive two hundred and thirty yards after she has taken six sloshes to cover fifty, I sometimes think that a new light comes into her eyes.'

'Exactly,' said the Sage.

* * * * * * * * *

From earliest youth (said the Oldest Member) Ramsden Waters had always been of a shrinking nature. He seemed permanently scared. Possibly his nurse had frightened him with tales of horror in his babyhood. If so, she must have been the Edgar Allan Poe of her sex, for, by the time he reached man's estate, Ramsden Waters had about as much ferocity and self-assertion as a blancmange. Even with other men he was noticeably timid, and with women he comported himself in a manner that roused their immediate scorn and antagonism. He was one of those men who fall over their feet and start apologizing for themselves the moment they see a woman. His idea of conversing with a girl was to perspire and tie himself into knots, making the while a strange gurgling sound like the language of some primitive tribe. If ever a remark of any coherence emerged from his tangled vocal cords it dealt with the weather, and he immediately apologized and qualified it. To such a man women are merciless, and it speedily became an article of faith with the feminine population of this locality that Ramsden Waters was an unfortunate incident and did not belong. Finally, after struggling for a time to keep up a connection in social circles, he gave it up and became a sort of hermit.

I think that caricature I just showed you weighed rather heavily on the poor fellow. Just as he was nerving himself to make another attempt to enter society, he would catch sight of it and say to himself, 'What hope is there for a man with a face like that?' These caricaturists are too ready to wound people simply in order to raise a laugh. Personally I am broad-minded enough to smile at that portrait of myself. It has given me great enjoyment, though why the committee permit it to— But then, of course, it isn't a bit like, whereas that of Ramsden Waters not only gave the man's exact appearance, very little exaggerated, but laid bare his very soul. That portrait is the portrait of a chump, and such Ramsden Waters undeniably was.

By the end of the first year in the neighbourhood, Ramsden, as I say, had become practically a hermit. He lived all by himself in a house near the fifteenth green, seeing nobody, going nowhere. His only solace was golf. His late father had given him an excellent education, and, even as early as his seventeenth year, I believe, he was going round difficult courses in par. Yet even this admirable gift, which might have done him social service, was rendered negligible by the fact that he was too shy and shrinking to play often with other men. As a rule, he confined himself to golfing by himself in the mornings and late evenings when the links were more or less deserted. Yes, in his twenty-ninth year, Ramsden Waters had sunk to the depth of becoming a secret golfer.

One lovely morning in summer, a scented morning of green and blue and gold, when the birds sang in the trees and the air had that limpid clearness which makes the first hole look about 100 yards long instead of 345, Ramsden Waters, alone as ever, stood on the first tee addressing his ball. For a space he waggled masterfully, then, drawing his club back with a crisp swish, brought it down. And, as he did so, a voice behind him cried:

'Bing!'

Ramsden's driver wobbled at the last moment. The ball flopped weakly among the trees on the right of the course. Ramsden turned to perceive, standing close beside him, a small, fat boy in a sailor suit. There was a pause.

'Rotten!' said the boy austerely.

Ramsden gulped. And then suddenly he saw that the boy was not alone. About a medium approach-putt distance, moving gracefully and languidly towards him, was a girl of such pronounced beauty that Ramsden Waters' heart looped the loop twice in rapid succession. It was the first time that he had seen Eunice Bray, and, like most men who saw her for the first time, he experienced the sensations of one in an express lift at the tenth floor going down who has left the majority of his internal organs up on the twenty-second. He felt a dazed emptiness. The world swam before his eyes.

You yourself saw Eunice just now; and, though you are in a sense immune, being engaged to a charming girl of your own, I noticed that you unconsciously braced yourself up and tried to look twice as handsome as nature ever intended you to. You smirked and, if you had a moustache, you would have twiddled it. You can imagine, then, the effect which this vision of loveliness had on lonely, diffident Ramsden Waters. It got right in amongst him.

'I'm afraid my little brother spoiled your stroke,' said Eunice. She did not speak at all apologetically, but rather as a goddess might have spoken to a swineherd.

Ramsden yammered noiselessly. As always in the presence of the opposite sex, and more than ever now, his vocal cords appeared to have tied themselves in a knot which would have baffled a sailor and might have perplexed Houdini. He could not even gargle.

'He is very fond of watching golf,' said the girl.

She took the boy by the hand, and was about to lead him off, when Ramsden miraculously recovered speech.

'Would he like to come round with me?' he croaked. How he had managed to acquire the nerve to make the suggestion he could never understand. I suppose that in certain supreme moments a sort of desperate recklessness descends on nervous men.

'How very kind of you!' said the girl indifferently. 'But I'm afraid—'

'I want to go!' shrilled the boy. 'I want to go!'

Fond as Eunice Bray was of her little brother, I imagine that the prospect of having him taken off her hands on a fine summer morning, when all nature urged her to sit in the shade on the terrace and read a book, was not unwelcome.

'It would be very kind of you if you would let him,' said Eunice. 'He wasn't able to go to the circus last week, and it was a great disappointment; this will do instead.'

She turned toward the terrace, and Ramsden, his head buzzing, tottered into the jungle to find his ball, followed by the boy.

I have never been able to extract full particulars of that morning's round from Ramsden. If you speak of it to him, he will wince and change the subject. Yet he seems to have had the presence of mind to pump Wilberforce as to the details of his home life, and by the end of the round he had learned that Eunice and her brother had just come to visit an aunt who lived in the neighbourhood. Their house was not far from the links; Eunice was not engaged to be married; and the aunt made a hobby of collecting dry seaweed, which she pressed and pasted in an album. One sometimes thinks that aunts live entirely for pleasure.

At the end of the round Ramsden staggered on to the terrace, tripping over his feet, and handed Wilberforce back in good condition. Eunice, who had just reached the chapter where the hero decides to give up all for love, thanked him perfunctorily without looking up from her book; and so ended the first spasm of Ramsden Waters' life romance.

There are few things more tragic than the desire of the moth for the star; and it is a curious fact that the spectacle of a star almost invariably fills the most sensible moth with thoughts above his station. No doubt, if Ramsden Waters had stuck around and waited long enough there might have come his way in the fullness of time some nice, homely girl with a squint and a good disposition who would have been about his form. In his modest day dreams he had aspired to nothing higher. But the sight of Eunice Bray seemed to have knocked all the sense out of the man. He must have known that he stood no chance of becoming anything to her other than a handy means of getting rid of little Wilberforce now and again. Why, the very instant that Eunice appeared in the place, every eligible bachelor for miles around her tossed his head with a loud, snorting sound, and galloped madly in her direction. Dashing young devils they were, handsome, well-knit fellows with the figures of Greek gods and the faces of movie heroes. Any one of them could have named his own price from the advertisers of collars. They were the sort of young men you see standing grandly beside the full-page picture of the seven-seater Magnifico car in the magazines. And it was against this field that Ramsden Waters, the man with the unshuffled face, dared to pit his feeble personality. One weeps.

Something of the magnitude of the task he had undertaken must have come home to Ramsden at a very early point in the proceedings. At Eunice's home, at the hour when women receive callers, he was from the start a mere unconsidered unit in the mob scene. While his rivals clustered thickly about the girl, he was invariably somewhere on the outskirts listening limply to the aunt. I imagine that seldom has any young man had such golden opportunities of learning all about dried seaweed. Indeed, by the end of the month Ramsden Waters could not have known more about seaweed if he had been a deep sea fish. And yet he was not happy. He was in a position, if he had been at a dinner party and things had got a bit slow, to have held the table spellbound with the first-hand information about dried seaweed, straight from the stable; yet nevertheless he chafed. His soul writhed and sickened within him. He lost weight and went right off his approach-shots. I confess that my heart bled for the man.

His only consolation was that nobody else, not even the fellows who worked their way right through the jam and got seats in the front row where they could glare into her eyes and hang on her lips and all that sort of thing, seemed to be making any better progress.

And so matters went on till one day Eunice decided to take up golf. Her motive for doing this was, I believe, simply because Kitty Manders, who had won a small silver cup at a monthly handicap, receiving thirty-six, was always dragging the conversation round to this trophy, and if there was one firm article in Eunice Bray's simple creed it was that she would be hanged if she let Kitty, who was by way of being a rival on a small scale, put anything over on her. I do not defend Eunice, but women are women, and I doubt if any of them really take up golf in that holy, quest-of-the-grail spirit which animates men. I have known girls to become golfers as an excuse for wearing pink jumpers, and one at least who did it because she had read in the beauty hints in the evening paper that it made you lissome. Girls will be girls.

Her first lessons Eunice received from the professional, but after that she saved money by distributing herself among her hordes of admirers, who were only too willing to give up good matches to devote themselves to her tuition. By degrees she acquired a fair skill and a confidence in her game which was not altogether borne out by results. From Ramsden Waters she did not demand a lesson. For one thing it never occurred to her that so poor-spirited a man could be of any use at the game, and for another Ramsden was always busy tooling round with little Wilberforce.

Yet it was with Ramsden that she was paired in the first competition for which she entered, the annual mixed foursomes. And it was on the same evening that the list of the draw went up on the notice board that Ramsden proposed.

The mind of a man in love works in strange ways. To you and to me there would seem to be no reason why the fact that Eunice's name and his own had been drawn out of a hat together should so impress Ramsden, but he looked on it as an act of God.

It seemed to him to draw them close together, to set up a sort of spiritual affinity. In a word, it acted on the poor fellow like a tonic, and that very night he went around to her house, and having, after a long and extremely interesting conversation with her aunt, contrived to get her alone, coughed eleven times in a strangled sort of way, and suggested that the wedding bells should ring out.

Eunice was more startled than angry.

'Of course, I'm tremendously complimented, Mr—' She had to pause to recall the name. 'Mr—'

'Waters,' said Ramsden, humbly.

'Of course, yes. Mr Waters. As I say, it's a great compliment—'

'Not at all!'

'A great compliment—'

'No, no!' murmured Ramsden obsequiously.

'I wish you wouldn't interrupt!' snapped Eunice with irritation. No girl likes to have to keep going back and trying over her speeches. 'It's a great compliment, but it is quite impossible.'

'Just as you say, of course,' agreed Ramsden.

'What,' demanded Eunice, 'have you to offer me? I don't mean money. I mean something more spiritual. What is there in you, Mr Walter—'

'Waters.'

'Mr Waters. What is there in you that would repay a girl for giving up the priceless boon of freedom?'

'I know a lot about dried seaweed,' suggested Ramsden hopefully.

Eunice shook her head.

'No,' she said, 'it is quite impossible. You have paid me the greatest compliment a man can pay a woman, Mr Waterson—'

'Waters,' said Ramsden. 'I'll write it down for you.'

'Please don't trouble. I am afraid we shall never meet again—'

'But we are partners in the mixed foursomes to-morrow.'

'Oh, yes, so we are!' said Eunice. 'Well, mind you play up. I want to win a cup more than anything on earth.'

'Ah!' said Ramsden, 'if only I could win what I want to win more than anything else on earth! You, I mean,' he added, to make his meaning clear. 'If I could win you—' His tongue tied itself in a bow knot round his uvula, and he could say no more. He moved slowly to the door, paused with his fingers on the handle for one last look over his shoulder, and walked silently into the cupboard where Eunice's aunt kept her collection of dried seaweed.

His second start was favoured with greater luck, and he found himself out in the hall, and presently in the cool air of the night, with the stars shining down on him. Had those silent stars ever shone down on a more broken-hearted man? Had the cool air of the night ever fanned a more fevered brow? Ah, yes! Or, rather, ah no!

There was not a very large entry for the mixed foursomes competition. In my experience there seldom is. Men are as a rule idealists, and wish to keep their illusions regarding women intact, and it is difficult for the most broad-minded man to preserve a chivalrous veneration for the sex after a woman has repeatedly sliced into the rough and left him a difficult recovery. Women, too – I am not speaking of the occasional champions, but of the average woman, the one with the handicap of 33, who plays in high-heeled shoes – are apt to giggle when they foozle out of a perfect lie, and this makes for misogyny. Only eight couples assembled on the tenth tee (where our foursome matches start) on the morning after Ramsden Waters had proposed to Eunice. Six of these were negligible, consisting of males of average skill and young women who played golf because it kept them out in the fresh air. Looking over the field, Ramsden felt that the only serious rivalry was to be feared from Marcella Bingley and her colleague, a 16-handicap youth named George Perkins, with whom they were paired for the opening round. George was a pretty indifferent performer, but Marcella, a weather-beaten female with bobbed hair and the wrists of a welterweight pugilist, had once appeared in the women's open championship and swung a nasty iron.

Ramsden watched her drive a nice, clean shot down the middle of the fairway, and spoke earnestly to Eunice. His heart was in this competition, for, though the first prize in the mixed foursomes does not perhaps entitle the winners to a place in the hall of fame, Ramsden had the soul of the true golfer. And the true golfer wants to win whenever he starts, whether he is playing in a friendly round or in the open championship.

'What we've got to do is to play steadily,' he said. 'Don't try any fancy shots. Go for safety. Miss Bingley is a tough proposition, but George Perkins is sure to foozle a few, and if we play safe we've got 'em cold. The others don't count.'

You notice something odd about this speech. Something in it strikes you as curious. Precisely. It affected Eunice Bray in the same fashion. In the first place, it contains forty-four words, some of them of two syllables, others of even greater length. In the second place, it was spoken crisply, almost commandingly, without any of that hesitation and stammering which usually characterized Ramsden Waters' utterances. Eunice was puzzled. She was also faintly resentful. True, there was not a word in what he had said that was calculated to bring the blush of shame to the cheek of modesty; nevertheless, she felt vaguely that Ramsden

Waters had exceeded the limits. She had been prepared for a gurgling Ramsden Waters, a Ramsden Waters who fell over his large feet and perspired; but here was a Ramsden Waters who addressed her not merely as an equal, but with more than a touch of superiority. She eyed him coldly, but he had turned to speak to little Wilberforce, who was to accompany them on the round.

'And you, my lad,' said Ramsden curtly, 'you kindly remember that this is a competition, and keep your merry flow of conversation as much as possible to yourself. You've got a bad habit of breaking into small talk when a man's addressing the ball.'

'If you think that my brother will be in the way—' began Eunice coldly.

'Oh, I don't mind him coming round,' said Ramsden, 'if he keeps quiet.'

Eunice gasped. She had not played enough golf to understand how that noblest of games changes a man's whole nature when on the links. She was thinking of something crushing to say to him, when he advanced to the tee to drive off.

He drove a perfect ball, hard and low with a lot of roll. Even Eunice was impressed.

'Good shot, partner!' she said.

Ramsden was apparently unaware that she had spoken. He was gazing down the fairway with his club over his left shoulder in an attitude almost identical with that of Sandy McBean in the plate labelled 'The Drive – Correct Finish', to face page twenty-four of his monumental work, 'How to Become a Scratch Player Your First Season by Studying Photographs'. Eunice bit her lip. She was piqued. She felt as if she had patted the head of a pet lamb, and the lamb had turned and bitten her in the finger.

'I said, "Good shot, partner!"' she repeated coldly.

'Yes,' said Ramsden, 'but don't talk. It prevents one concentrating.' He turned to Wilberforce. 'And don't let me have to tell you that again!' he said.

'Wilberforce has been like a mouse!'

'That is what I complain of,' said Ramsden. 'Mice make a beastly scratching sound, and that's what he was doing when I drove that ball.'

'He was only playing with the sand in the tee box.'

'Well, if he does it again, I shall be reluctantly compelled to take steps.'

They walked in silence to where the ball had stopped. It was nicely perched up on the grass, and to have plunked it on to the green with an iron should have been for any reasonable golfer the work of a moment. Eunice, however, only succeeded in slicing it feebly into the rough.

Ramsden reached for his niblick and plunged into the bushes. And, presently, as if it had been shot up by some convulsion of nature, the ball, accompanied on the early stages of its journey by about a pound of mixed mud, grass, and pebbles, soared through the air and fell on the green. But the mischief had been done. Miss Bingley, putting forcefully, put the opposition ball down for a four and won the hole.

Eunice now began to play better, and, as Ramsden was on the top of his game, a ding-dong race ensued for the remainder of the first nine holes. The Bingley–Perkins combination, owing to some inspired work by the female of the species, managed to keep their lead up to the tricky ravine hole, but there George Perkins, as might have been expected of him, deposited the ball right in among the rocks, and Ramsden and Eunice drew level. The next four holes were halved and they reached the club-house with no advantage to either side. Here there was a pause while Miss Bingley went to the professional's shop to have a tack put into the leather of her mashie, which had worked loose. George Perkins and little Wilberforce, who believed in keeping up their strength, melted silently away in the direction of the refreshment bar, and Ramsden and Eunice were alone.

The pique which Eunice had felt at the beginning of the game had vanished by now. She was feeling extremely pleased with her performance on the last few holes, and would have been glad to go into the matter fully. Also, she was conscious of a feeling not perhaps of respect so much as condescending tolerance towards Ramsden. He might be a pretty minus quantity in a drawing-room or at a dance, but in a bunker or out in the open with a cleek, Eunice felt, you'd be surprised. She was just about to address him in a spirit of kindliness, when he spoke.

'Better keep your brassey in the bag on the next nine,' he said. 'Stick to the iron. The great thing is to keep 'em straight!'

Eunice gasped. Indeed, had she been of a less remarkable beauty one would have said that she snorted. The sky turned black, and all her amiability was swept away in a flood of fury. The blood left her face and surged back in a rush of crimson. You are engaged to be married and I take it that there exists between you and your *fiancée* the utmost love and trust and understanding; but would you have the nerve, could you summon up the cold, callous gall to tell your Genevieve that she wasn't capable of using her wooden clubs? I think not. Yet this was what Ramsden Waters had told Eunice, and the delicately nurtured girl staggered before the coarse insult. Her refined, sensitive nature was all churned up.

Ever since she had made her first drive at golf, she had prided herself on her use of the wood. Her brother and her brassey were the only things she loved. And here was this man deliberately... Eunice choked.

'Mr Waters!'

Before they could have further speech George Perkins and little Wilberforce ambled in a bloated way out of the club-house.

'I've had three ginger-ales,' observed the boy. 'Where do we go from here?'

'Our honour,' said Ramsden. 'Shoot!'

Eunice took out her driver without a word. Her little figure was tense with emotion. She swung vigorously, and pulled the ball far out on to the fairway of the ninth hole.

'Even off the tee,' said Ramsden, 'you had better use an iron. You must keep 'em straight.'

Their eyes met. Hers were glittering with the fury of a woman scorned. His were cold and hard. And, suddenly, as she looked at his awful, pale, set golf face, something seemed to snap in Eunice. A strange sensation of weakness and humility swept over her. So might the cave woman have felt when, with her back against a cliff and unable to dodge, she watched her suitor take his club in the interlocking grip, and, after a preliminary waggle, start his back-swing.

The fact was that, all her life, Eunice had been accustomed to the homage of men. From the time she had put her hair up every man she had met had grovelled before her, and she had acquired a mental attitude toward the other sex which was a blend of indifference and contempt. For the cringing specimens who curled up and died all over the hearth rug if she spoke a cold word to them she had nothing but scorn. She dreamed wistfully of those brusque cavemen of whom she read in the novels which she took out of the village circulating library. The female novelist who was at that time her favourite always supplied with each chunk of wholesome and invigorating fiction one beetle-browed hero with a grouch and a scowl, who rode wild horses over the countryside till they foamed at the mouth, and treated women like dirt. That, Eunice had thought yearningly, as she talked to youths whose spines turned to gelatine at one glance from her bright eyes, was the sort of man she wanted to meet and never seemed to come across.

Of all the men whose acquaintance she had made recently she had despised Ramsden Waters most. Where others had grovelled he had tied himself into knots. Where others had gazed at her like sheep he had goggled at her like a kicked spaniel. She had only permitted him to hang round because he seemed so fond of little Wilberforce. And here he was, ordering her about and piercing her with gimlet eyes, for all the world as if he were Claude Delamere, in the thirty-second chapter of 'The Man of Chilled Steel', the one where Claude drags Lady Matilda around the smoking-room by her hair because she gave the rose from her bouquet to the Italian count.

She was half-cowed, half-resentful.

'Mr Winklethorpe told me I was very good with the wooden clubs,' she said defiantly.

'He's a great kidder,' said Ramsden.

He went down the hill to where his ball lay. Eunice proceeded direct for the green. Much as she told herself that she hated this man, she never questioned his ability to get there with his next shot.

George Perkins, who had long since forfeited any confidence which his partner might have reposed in him, had topped his drive, leaving Miss Bingley a difficult second out of a sandy ditch. The hole was halved.

The match went on. Ramsden won the short hole, laying his ball dead with a perfect iron shot, but at the next, the long dog-leg hole, Miss Bingley regained the honour. They came to the last all square.

As the match had started on the tenth tee, the last hole to be negotiated was, of course, what in the ordinary run of human affairs is the ninth, possibly the trickiest on the course. As you know, it is necessary to carry with one's initial wallop that combination of stream and lake into which so many well-meant drives have flopped. This done, the player proceeds up the face of a steep slope, to find himself ultimately on a green which looks like the sea in the storm scene of a melodrama. It heaves and undulates, and is altogether a nasty thing to have happen to one at the end of a gruelling match. But it is the first shot, the drive, which is the real test, for the water and the trees form a mental hazard of unquestionable toughness.

George Perkins, as he addressed his ball for the vital stroke, manifestly wobbled. He was scared to the depths of his craven soul. He tried to pray, but all he could remember was the hymn for those in peril on the deep, into which category, he feared, his ball would shortly fall. Breathing a few bars of this, he swung. There was a musical click, and the ball, singing over the water like a bird, breasted the hill like a homing aeroplane and fell in the centre of the fairway within easy distance of the plateau green.

'Nice work, partner,' said Miss Bingley, speaking for the first and last time in the course of the proceedings.

George unravelled himself with a modest simper. He felt like a gambler who has placed his all on a number at roulette and sees the white ball tumble into the correct compartment.

Eunice moved to the tee. In the course of the last eight holes the girl's haughty soul had been rudely harrowed. She had foozled two drives and three approach-shots and had missed a short putt on the last green but three. She had that consciousness of sin which afflicts the golfer off his game, that curious self-loathing which humbles the proudest. Her knees felt weak and all nature seemed to bellow at her that this was where she was going to blow up with a loud report.

Even as her driver rose above her shoulder she was acutely aware that she was making eighteen out of the twenty-three errors which complicate the drive at golf. She knew that her head had swayed like some beautiful flower in a stiff breeze. The heel of her left foot was pointing down the course. Her grip had shifted, and her wrists felt like sticks of boiled asparagus. As the club began to descend she perceived that she had underestimated the total of her errors. And when the ball, badly topped, bounded down the slope and entered the muddy water like a timid diver on a cold morning she realized that she had a full hand. There are twenty-three things which it is possible to do wrong in the drive, and she had done them all.

Silently Ramsden Waters made a tee and placed thereon a new ball. He was a golfer who rarely despaired, but he was playing three, and his opponents' ball would undoubtedly be on the green, possibly even dead, in two. Nevertheless, perhaps, by a supreme drive, and one or two miracles later on, the game might be saved. He concentrated his whole soul on the ball.

I need scarcely tell you that Ramsden Waters pressed....

Swish came the driver. The ball, fanned by the wind, rocked a little on the tee, then settled down in its original position.

Ramsden Waters, usually the most careful of players, had missed the globe.

For a moment there was a silence – a silence which Ramsden had to strive with an effort almost physically painful not to break. Rich oaths surged to his lips, and blistering maledictions crashed against the back of his clenched teeth.

The silence was broken by little Wilberforce.

One can only gather that there lurks in the supposedly innocuous amber of ginger-ale an elevating something which the temperance reformers have overlooked. Wilberforce Bray had, if you remember, tucked away no fewer than three in the spot where they would do most good. One presumes that the child, with all that stuff surging about inside him, had become thoroughly above himself. He uttered a merry laugh.

'Never hit it!' said little Wilberforce.

He was kneeling beside the tee box as he spoke, and now, as one who has seen all that there is to be seen and turns, sated, to other amusements, he moved round and began to play with the sand. The spectacle of his alluring trouser seat was one which a stronger man would have found it hard to resist. To Ramsden Waters it had the aspect of a formal invitation. For one moment his number 11 golf shoe, as supplied to all the leading professionals, wavered in mid-air, then crashed home.

Eunice screamed.

'How dare you kick my brother!'

Ramsden faced her, stern and pale.

'Madam,' he said, 'in similar circumstances I would have kicked the Archangel Gabriel!'

Then, stooping to his ball, he picked it up.

'The match is yours,' he said to Miss Bingley, who, having

paid no attention at all to the drama which had just concluded, was practising short chip shots with her mashie-niblick.

He bowed coldly to Eunice, cast one look of sombre satisfaction at little Wilberforce, who was painfully extricating himself from a bed of nettles into which he had rolled, and strode off. He crossed the bridge over the water and stalked up the hill.

Eunice watched him go, spellbound. Her momentary spurt of wrath at the kicking of her brother had died away, and she wished she had thought of doing it herself.

How splendid he looked, she felt, as she watched Ramsden striding up to the club-house – just like Carruthers Mordyke after he had flung Ermyntrude Vanstone from him in chapter forty-one of 'Gray Eyes That Gleam'. Her whole soul went out to him. This was the sort of man she wanted as a partner in life. How grandly he would teach her to play golf. It had sickened her when her former instructors, prefacing their criticism with glutinous praise, had mildly suggested that some people found it a good thing to keep the head still when driving and that though her methods were splendid it might be worth trying. They had spoken of her keeping her eye on the ball as if she were doing the ball a favour. What she wanted was a great, strong, rough brute of a fellow who would tell her not to move her damned head; a rugged Viking of a chap who, if she did not keep her eye on the ball, would black it for her. And Ramsden Waters was such a one. He might not look like a Viking, but after all it is the soul that counts, and as this afternoon's experience had taught her, Ramsden Waters had a soul that seemed to combine in equal proportions the outstanding characteristics of Nero, a wildcat, and the second mate of a tramp steamer.

* * * * * * * * *

That night Ramsden Waters sat in his study, a prey to the gloomiest emotions. The golf had died out of him by now, and he was reproaching himself bitterly for having ruined forever his chance of winning the only girl he had ever loved. How could she forgive him for his brutality? How could she overlook treatment which would have caused comment in the stokehold of a cattle ship? He groaned and tried to forget his sorrows by forcing himself to read.

But the choicest thoughts of the greatest writers had no power to grip him. He tried Vardon 'On the Swing', and the words swam before his eyes. He turned to Taylor 'On the Chip Shot', and the master's pure style seemed laboured and involved. He found solace neither in Braid 'On the Pivot' nor in Duncan 'On the Divot'. He was just about to give it up and go to bed though it was only nine o'clock, when the telephone bell rang.

'Hello!'

'Is that you, Mr Waters? This is Eunice Bray.' The receiver shook in Ramsden's hand. 'I've just remembered. Weren't we talking about something last night? Didn't you ask me to marry you or something? I know it was something.'

Ramsden gulped three times.

'I did,' he replied hollowly.

'We didn't settle anything, did we?'

'Eh?'

'I say, we sort of left it kind of open.'

'Yuk!'

'Well, would it bore you awfully,' said Eunice's soft voice, 'to come round now and go on talking it over?'

Ramsden tottered.

'We shall be quite alone,' said Eunice. 'Little Wilberforce has gone to bed with a headache.'

Ramsden paused a moment to disentangle his tongue from the back of his neck.

'I'll be right over!' he said huskily.

PROLOGUE

After we had sent in our card and waited for a few hours in the marbled ante-room, a bell rang and the major-domo, parting the priceless curtains, ushered us in to where the editor sat writing at his desk. We advanced on all fours, knocking our head reverently on the Aubusson carpet.

'Well?' he said at length, laying down his jewelled pen.

'We just looked in,' we said, humbly, 'to ask if it would be all right if we sent you an historical story.'

'The public does not want historical stories,' he said, frowning coldly.

'Ah, but the public hasn't seen one of ours!' we replied.

The editor placed a cigarette in a holder presented to him by a reigning monarch, and lit it with a match from a golden box, the gift of the millionaire president of the Amalgamated League of Working Plumbers.

'What this magazine requires,' he said, 'is red-blooded, one-hundred-per-cent dynamic stuff, palpitating with warm human interest and containing a strong, poignant love-motive.'

'That,' we replied, 'is us all over, Mabel.'

'What I need at the moment, however, is a golf story.'

'By a singular coincidence, ours is a golf story.'

'Ha! say you so?' said the editor, a flicker of interest passing over his finely-chiselled features. 'Then you may let me see it.'

He kicked us in the face, and we withdrew.

* * * * * * * * *

THE STORY

On the broad terrace outside his palace, overlooking the fair expanse of the Royal gardens, King Merolchazzar of Oom stood leaning on the low parapet, his chin in his hand and a frown on his noble face. The day was fine, and a light breeze bore up to him from the garden below a fragrant scent of flowers. But, for all the pleasure it seemed to give him, it might have been bone-fertilizer.

The fact is, King Merolchazzar was in love, and his suit was not prospering. Enough to upset any man.

Royal love affairs in those days were conducted on the correspondence system. A monarch, hearing good reports of a neighbouring princess, would despatch messengers with gifts to her Court, beseeching an interview. The Princess would name a date, and a formal meeting would take place; after which everything usually buzzed along pretty smoothly. But in the case of King Merolchazzar's courtship of the Princess of the Outer Isles there had been a regrettable hitch. She had acknowledged the gifts, saying that they were just what she had wanted and how had he guessed, and had added that, as regarded a meeting, she would let him know later. Since that day no word had come from her, and a gloomy spirit prevailed in the capital. At the Courtiers' Club, the meeting-place of the aristocracy of Oom, five to one in *pazazas* was freely offered against Merolchazzar's chances, but found no takers; while in the taverns of the common people, where less conservative odds were always to be had, you could get a snappy hundred to eight. 'For in good sooth,' writes a chronicler of the time on a half-brick and a couple of paving-stones which have survived to this day, 'it did indeed begin to appear as though our beloved monarch, the son of the sun and the nephew of the moon, had been handed the bitter fruit of the citron.'

The quaint old idiom is almost untranslatable, but one sees what he means.

* * * * * * * * *

As the King stood sombrely surveying the garden, his attention was attracted by a small, bearded man with bushy eyebrows and a face like a walnut, who stood not far away on a gravelled path flanked by rose bushes. For some minutes he eyed this man in silence, then he called to the Grand Vizier, who was standing in the little group of courtiers and officials at the other end of the terrace. The bearded man, apparently unconscious of the Royal scrutiny, had placed a rounded stone on the gravel, and was standing beside it making curious passes over it with his hoe. It was this singular behaviour that had attracted the King's attention. Superficially it seemed silly, and yet Merolchazzar had a curious feeling that there was a deep, even a holy, meaning behind the action.

'Who,' he inquired, 'is that?'

'He is one of your Majesty's gardeners,' replied the Vizier.

'I don't remember seeing him before. Who is he?'

The Vizier was a kind-hearted man, and he hesitated for a moment.

'It seems a hard thing to say of anyone, your Majesty,' he replied, 'but he is a Scotsman. One of your Majesty's invincible admirals recently made a raid on the inhospitable coast of that country at a spot known to the natives as S'nandrews and brought away this man.'

'What does he think he's doing?' asked the King, as the bearded one slowly raised the hoe above his right shoulder, slightly bending the left knee as he did so.

'It is some species of savage religious ceremony, your Majesty. According to the admiral, the dunes by the seashore where he landed were covered with a multitude of men behaving just as this man is doing. They had sticks in their hands, and they struck with these at small round objects. And every now and again—'

'Fo-o-ore!' called a gruff voice from below.

'And every now and again,' went on the Vizier, 'they would utter the strange melancholy cry which you have just heard. It is a species of chant.'

The Vizier broke off. The hoe had descended on the stone, and the stone, rising in a graceful arc, had sailed through the air and fallen within a foot of where the King stood.

'Hi!' exclaimed the Vizier.

The man looked up.

'You mustn't do that! You nearly hit his serene graciousness the King!'

'Mphm!' said the bearded man, nonchalantly, and began to wave his hoe mystically over another stone.

Into the King's careworn face there had crept a look of interest, almost of excitement.

'What god does he hope to propitiate by these rites?' he asked.

'The deity, I learn from your Majesty's admiral, is called Gowf.'

'Gowf? Gowf?' King Merolchazzar ran over in his mind the muster-roll of the gods of Oom. There were sixty-seven of them, but Gowf was not of their number. 'It is a strange religion,' he murmured. 'A strange religion, indeed. But, by Belus, distinctly attractive. I have an idea that Oom could do with a religion like that. It has a zip to it. A sort of fascination, if you know what I mean. It looks to me extraordinarily like what the Court physician ordered. I will talk to this fellow and learn more of these holy ceremonies.'

And, followed by the Vizier, the King made his way into the garden. The Vizier was now in a state of some apprehension. He was exercised in his mind as to the effect which the embracing of a new religion by the King might have on the formidable Church party. It would be certain to cause displeasure among the priesthood; and in those days it was a ticklish business to offend the priesthood, even for a monarch. And, if Merolchazzar had a fault, it was a tendency to be a little tactless in his dealings with that powerful body. Only a few mornings back the High Priest of Hec had taken the Vizier aside to complain about the quality of the meat which the King had been using lately for his sacrifices. He might be a child in worldly matters, said the High Priest, but if the King supposed that he did not know the difference between home-grown domestic and frozen imported foreign, it was time his Majesty was disabused of the idea. If, on top of this little unpleasantness, King Merolchazzar were to become an adherent of this new Gowf, the Vizier did not know what might not happen.

The King stood beside the bearded foreigner, watching him closely. The second stone soared neatly on to the terrace. Merolchazzar uttered an excited cry. His eyes were glowing, and he breathed quickly.

'It doesn't look difficult,' he muttered.

'Hoots!' said the bearded man.

'I believe I could do it,' went on the King, feverishly. 'By the eight green gods of the mountain, I believe I could! By the holy fire that burns night and day before the altar of Belus, I'm *sure* I could! By Hec, I'm going to do it now! Gimme that hoe!'

'Toots!' said the bearded man.

It seemed to the King that the fellow spoke derisively, and his blood boiled angrily. He seized the hoe and raised it above his shoulder, bracing himself solidly on widely-parted feet. His pose was an exact reproduction of the one in which the Court sculptor had depicted him when working on the life-size statue ('Our Athletic King') which stood in the principal square of the city; but it did not impress the stranger. He uttered a discordant laugh.

'Ye puir gonuph!' he cried, 'whit kin' o' a staunce is that?'

The King was hurt. Hitherto the attitude had been generally admired.

'It's the way I always stand when killing lions,' he said. '"In killing lions,"' he added, quoting from the well-known treatise of Nimrod, the recognized text-book on the sport, '"the weight at the top of the swing should be evenly balanced on both feet."'

'Ah, weel, ye're no killing lions the noo. Ye're gowfing.'

A sudden humility descended upon the King. He felt, as so many men were to feel in similar circumstances in ages to come, as though he were a child looking eagerly for guidance to an all-wise master – a child, moreover, handicapped by water on the brain, feet three sizes too large for him, and hands consisting mainly of thumbs.

'O thou of noble ancestors and agreeable disposition!' he said, humbly. 'Teach me the true way.'

'Use the interlocking grup and keep the staunce a wee bit open and slow back, and dinna press or sway the heid and keep yer e'e on the ba'.'

'My which on the what?' said the King, bewildered.

'I fancy, your Majesty,' hazarded the Vizier, 'that he is respectfully suggesting that your serene graciousness should deign to keep your eye on the ball.'

'Oh, ah!' said the King.

The first golf lesson ever seen in the kingdom of Oom had begun.

* * * * * * * * *

Up on the terrace, meanwhile, in the little group of courtiers and officials, a whispered consultation was in progress. Officially, the King's unfortunate love affair was supposed to be a strict secret. But you know how it is. These things get about. The Grand Vizier tells the Lord High Chamberlain; the Lord High Chamberlain whispers it in confidence to the Supreme Hereditary Custodian of the Royal Pet Dog; the Supreme Hereditary Custodian hands it on to the Exalted Overseer of the King's Wardrobe on the understanding that it is to go no farther; and, before you know where you are, the varlets and scurvy knaves are gossiping about it in the kitchens, and the Society journalists have started to carve it out on bricks for the next issue of *Palace Prattlings*.

'The long and short of it is,' said the Exalted Overseer of the King's Wardrobe, 'we must cheer him up.'

There was a murmur of approval. In those days of easy executions it was no light matter that a monarch should be a prey to gloom.

'But how?' queried the Lord High Chamberlain.

'I know,' said the Supreme Hereditary Custodian of the Royal Pet Dog. 'Try him with the minstrels.'

'Here! Why us?' protested the leader of the minstrels.

'Don't be silly!' said the Lord High Chamberlain. 'It's for your good just as much as ours. He was asking only last night why he never got any music nowadays. He told me to find out whether you supposed he paid you simply to eat and sleep, because if so he knew what to do about it.'

'Oh, in that case!' The leader of the minstrels started nervously. Collecting his assistants and tiptoeing down the garden, he took up his stand a few feet in Merolchazzar's rear, just as that much-enduring monarch, after twenty-five futile attempts, was once more addressing his stone.

Lyric writers in those days had not reached the supreme pitch of excellence which has been produced by modern musical comedy. The art was in its infancy then, and the best the minstrels could do was this – and they did it just as Merolchazzar, raising the hoe with painful care, reached the top of his swing and started down: –

'Oh, tune the string and let us sing
Our godlike, great, and glorious King!
He's a bear! He's a bear! He's a bear!'

There were sixteen more verses, touching on their ruler's prowess in the realms of sport and war, but they were not destined to be sung on that circuit. King Merolchazzar jumped like a stung bullock, lifted his head, and missed the globe for the twenty-sixth time. He spun round on the minstrels, who were working pluckily through their song of praise: –

'Oh, may his triumphs never cease!
He has the strength of ten!
First in war, first in peace,
First in the hearts of his countrymen.'

'Get out!' roared the King.

'Your Majesty?' quavered the leader of the minstrels.

'Make a noise like an egg and beat it!' (Again one finds the chronicler's idiom impossible to reproduce in modern speech, and must be content with a literal translation.) 'By the bones of my ancestors, it's a little hard! By the beard of the sacred goat, it's tough! What in the name of Belus and Hec do you mean, you yowling misfits, by starting that sort of stuff when a man's swinging? I was just shaping to hit it right that time when you butted in, you—'

The minstrels melted away. The bearded man patted the fermenting monarch paternally on the shoulder.

'Ma mannie,' he said, 'ye may no' be a gowfer yet, but hoots! ye're learning the language fine!'

King Merolchazzar's fury died away. He simpered modestly at these words of commendation, the first his bearded preceptor had uttered. With exemplary patience he turned to address the stone for the twenty-seventh time.

That night it was all over the city that the King had gone crazy over a new religion, and the orthodox shook their heads.

* * * * * * * * *

We of the present day, living in the midst of a million marvels of a complex civilization, have learned to adjust ourselves to conditions and to take for granted phenomena which in an earlier and less advanced age would have caused the profoundest excitement and even alarm. We accept without comment the telephone, the automobile, and the wireless telegraph, and we are unmoved by the spectacle of our fellow-human beings in the grip of the first stages of golf fever. Far otherwise was it with the courtiers and officials about the Palace of Oom. The obsession of the King was the sole topic of conversation.

Every day now, starting forth at dawn and returning only with the falling of darkness, Merolchazzar was out on the Linx, as the outdoor temple of the new god was called. In a luxurious house adjoining this expanse the bearded Scotsman had been installed, and there he could be found at almost any hour of the day fashioning out of holy wood the weird implements indispensable to the new religion. As a recognition of his services, the King had bestowed upon him a large pension, innumerable *kaddiz* or slaves, and the title of Promoter of the King's Happiness, which for the sake of convenience was generally shortened to The Pro.

At present, Oom being a conservative country, the worship of the new god had not attracted the public in great numbers. In fact, except for the Grand Vizier, who, always a faithful follower of his sovereign's fortunes, had taken to Gowf from the start, the courtiers held aloof to a man. But the Vizier had thrown himself into the new worship with such vigour and earnestness that it was not long before he won from the King the title of Supreme Splendiferous Maintainer of the Twenty-Four Handicap Except on Windy Days when It Goes Up to Thirty – a title which in ordinary conversation was usually abbreviated to The Dub.

All these new titles, it should be said, were, so far as the courtiers were concerned, a fruitful source of discontent. There were black looks and mutinous whispers. The laws of precedence were being disturbed, and the courtiers did not like it. It jars a man who for years has had his social position all cut and dried – a man, to take an instance at random, who, as Second

Deputy Shiner of the Royal Hunting Boots, knows that his place is just below the Keeper of the Eel-Hounds and just above the Second Tenor of the Corps of Minstrels – it jars him, we say, to find suddenly that he has got to go down a step in favour of the Hereditary Bearer of the King's Baffy.

But it was from the priesthood that the real, serious opposition was to be expected. And the priests of the sixty-seven gods of Oom were up in arms. As the white-bearded High Priest of Hec, who, by virtue of his office was generally regarded as leader of the guild, remarked in a glowing speech at an extraordinary meeting of the Priests' Equity Association, he had always set his face against the principle of the Closed Shop hitherto, but there were moments when every thinking man had to admit that enough was sufficient, and it was his opinion that such a moment had now arrived. The cheers which greeted the words showed how correctly he had voiced popular sentiment.

* * * * * * * * *

Of all those who had listened to the High Priest's speech, none had listened more intently than the King's half-brother, Ascobaruch. A sinister, disappointed man, this Ascobaruch, with mean eyes and a crafty smile. All his life he had been consumed with ambition, and until now it had looked as though he must go to his grave with this ambition unfulfilled. All his life he had wanted to be King of Oom, and now he began to see daylight. He was sufficiently versed in Court intrigues to be aware that the priests were the party that really counted, the source from which all successful revolutions sprang. And of all the priests the one that mattered most was the venerable High Priest of Hec.

It was to this prelate, therefore, that Ascobaruch made his way at the close of the proceedings. The meeting had dispersed after passing a unanimous vote of censure on King Merolchazzar, and the High Priest was refreshing himself in the vestry – for the meeting had taken place in the Temple of Hec – with a small milk and honey.

'Some speech!' began Ascobaruch in his unpleasant, crafty way. None knew better than he the art of appealing to human vanity.

The High Priest was plainly gratified.

'Oh, I don't know,' he said, modestly.

'Yessir!' said Ascobaruch. 'Considerable oration! What I can never understand is how you think up all these things to say. I couldn't do it if you paid me. The other night I had to propose the Visitors at the Old Alumni dinner of Oom University, and my mind seemed to go all blank. But you just stand up and the words come fluttering out of you like bees out of a barn. I simply cannot understand it. The thing gets past me.'

'Oh, it's just a knack.'

'A divine gift, I should call it.'

'Perhaps you're right,' said the High Priest, finishing his milk and honey. He was wondering why he had never realized before what a capital fellow Ascobaruch was.

'Of course,' went on Ascobaruch, 'you had an excellent subject. I mean to say, inspiring and all that. Why, by Hec, even I – though, of course, I couldn't have approached your level – even I could have done something with a subject like that. I mean, going off and worshipping a new god no one has ever heard of. I tell you, my blood fairly boiled. Nobody has a greater respect and esteem for Merolchazzar than I have, but I mean to say, what! Not right, I mean, going off worshipping gods no one has ever heard of! I'm a peaceable man, and I've made it a rule never to mix in politics, but if you happened to say to me as we were sitting here, just as one reasonable man to another – if you happened to say, "Ascobaruch, I think it's time that definite steps were taken," I should reply frankly, "My dear old High Priest, I absolutely agree with you, and I'm with you all the way." You might even go so far as to suggest that the only way out of the muddle was to assassinate Merolchazzar and start with a clean slate.'

The High Priest stroked his beard thoughtfully.

'I am bound to say I never thought of going quite so far as that.'

'Merely a suggestion, of course,' said Ascobaruch. 'Take it or leave it. I shan't be offended. If you know a superior excavation, go to it. But as a sensible man – and I've always maintained that you are the most sensible man in the country – you must see that it would be a solution. Merolchazzar has been a pretty good king, of course. No one denies that. A fair general, no doubt, and a plus-man at lion-hunting. But, after all – look at it fairly – is life all battles and lion-hunting? Isn't there a deeper side? Wouldn't it be better for the country to have some good orthodox fellow who has worshipped Hec all his life, and could be relied on to maintain the old beliefs – wouldn't the fact that a man like that was on the throne be likely to lead to more general prosperity? There are dozens of men of that kind simply waiting to be asked. Let us say, purely for purposes of argument, that you approached *me*. I should reply, "Unworthy though I know myself to be of such an honour, I can tell you this. If you put me on the throne, you can bet your bottom *pazaza* that there's one thing that won't suffer, and that is the worship of Hec!" That's the way I feel about it.'

The High Priest pondered.

'O thou of unshuffled features but amiable disposition!' he said, 'thy discourse soundeth good to me. Could it be done?'

'Could it!' Ascobaruch uttered a hideous laugh. 'Could it! Arouse me in the night-watches and ask me! Question me on the matter, having stopped me for that purpose on the public highway! What I would suggest – I'm not dictating, mind you; merely trying to help you out – what I would suggest is that you took that long, sharp knife of yours, the one you use for the sacrifices, and toddled out to the Linx – you're sure to find the King there; and just when he's raising that sacrilegious stick of his over his shoulder—'

'O man of infinite wisdom,' cried the High Priest, warmly, 'verily hast thou spoken a fullness of the mouth!'

'Is it a wager?' said Ascobaruch.

'It is a wager!' said the High Priest.

'That's that, then,' said Ascobaruch. 'Now, I don't want to be mixed up in any unpleasantness, so what I think I'll do while what you might call the preliminaries are being arranged is to go and take a little trip abroad somewhere. The Middle Lakes are pleasant at this time of year. When I come back, it's possible that all the formalities will have been completed, yes?'

'Rely on me, by Hec!' said the High Priest grimly, as he fingered his weapon.

* * * * * * * * *

The High Priest was as good as his word. Early on the morrow he made his way to the Linx, and found the King holing-out on the second green. Merolchazzar was in high good humour.

'Greetings, O venerable one!' he cried, jovially. 'Hadst thou come a moment sooner, thou wouldst have seen me lay my ball dead – aye, dead as mutton, with the sweetest little half-mashie-niblick chip-shot ever seen outside the sacred domain of S'nandrew, on whom' – he bared his head reverently

– 'be peace! In one under bogey did I do the hole – yea, and that despite the fact that, slicing my drive, I became ensnared in yonder undergrowth.'

The High Priest had not the advantage of understanding one word of what the King was talking about, but he gathered with satisfaction that Merolchazzar was pleased and wholly without suspicion. He clasped an unseen hand more firmly about the handle of his knife, and accompanied the monarch to the next altar. Merolchazzar stooped, and placed a small round white object on a little mound of sand. In spite of his austere views, the High Priest, always a keen student of ritual, became interested.

'Why does your Majesty do that?'

'I tee it up that it may fly the fairer. If I did not, then would it be apt to run along the ground like a beetle instead of soaring like a bird, and mayhap, for thou seest how rough and tangled is the grass before us, I should have to use a niblick for my second.'

The High Priest groped for his meaning.

'It is a ceremony to propitiate the god and bring good luck?'

'You might call it that.'

The High Priest shook his head.

'I may be old-fashioned,' he said, 'but I should have thought that, to propitiate a god, it would have been better to have sacrificed one of these *kaddiz* on his altar.'

'I confess,' replied the King, thoughtfully, 'that I have often felt that it would be a relief to one's feelings to sacrifice one or two *kaddiz*, but The Pro for some reason or other has set his face against it.' He swung at the ball, and sent it forcefully down the fairway. 'By Abe, the son of Mitchell,' he cried, shading his eyes, 'a bird of a drive! How truly is it written in the book of the prophet Vadun, "The left hand applieth the force, the right doth but guide. Grip not, therefore, too closely with the right hand!" Yesterday I was pulling all the time.'

The High Priest frowned.

'It is written in the sacred book of Hec, your Majesty, "Thou shalt not follow after strange gods."'

'Take thou this stick, O venerable one,' said the King, paying no attention to the remark, 'and have a shot thyself. True, thou art well stricken in years, but many a man has so wrought that he was able to give his grandchildren a stroke a hole. It is never too late to begin.'

The High Priest shrank back, horrified. The King frowned.

'It is our Royal wish,' he said, coldly.

The High Priest was forced to comply. Had they been alone, it is possible that he might have risked all on one swift stroke with his knife, but by this time a group of *kaddiz* had drifted up, and were watching the proceedings with that supercilious detachment so characteristic of them. He took the stick and arranged his limbs as the King directed.

'Now,' said Merolchazzar, 'slow back and keep your e'e on the ba'!'

* * * * * * * * *

A month later, Ascobaruch returned from his trip. He had received no word from the High Priest announcing the success of the revolution, but there might be many reasons for that. It was with unruffled contentment that he bade his charioteer drive him to the palace. He was glad to get back, for after all a holiday is hardly a holiday if you have left your business affairs unsettled.

As he drove, the chariot passed a fair open space, on the outskirts of the city. A sudden chill froze the serenity of Ascobaruch's mood. He prodded the charioteer sharply in the small of the back.

'What is that?' he demanded, catching his breath.

All over the green expanse could be seen men in strange robes, moving to and fro in couples and bearing in their hands mystic wands. Some searched restlessly in the bushes, others were walking briskly in the direction of small red flags. A sickening foreboding of disaster fell upon Ascobaruch.

The charioteer seemed surprised at the question.

'Yon's the muneecipal linx,' he replied.

'The what?'

'The muneecipal linx.'

'Tell me, fellow, why do you talk that way?'

'Whit way?'

'Why, like that. The way you're talking.'

'Hoots, mon!' said the charioteer. 'His Majesty King Merolchazzar – may his handicap decrease! – hae passit a law that a' his soobjects shall do it. Aiblins, 'tis the language spoken by The Pro, on whom be peace! Mphm!'

Ascobaruch sat back limply, his head swimming. The chariot drove on, till now it took the road adjoining the royal Linx. A wall lined a portion of this road, and suddenly, from behind this wall, there rent the air a great shout of laughter.

'Pull up!' cried Ascobaruch to the charioteer.

He had recognized that laugh. It was the laugh of Merolchazzar.

Ascobaruch crept to the wall and cautiously poked his head over it. The sight he saw drove the blood from his face and left him white and haggard.

The King and the Grand Vizier were playing a foursome against the Pro and the High Priest of Hec, and the Vizier had just laid the High Priest a dead stymie.

Ascobaruch tottered to the chariot.

'Take me back,' he muttered, pallidly. 'I've forgotten something!'

*   *   *   *   *   *   *   *   *

And so golf came to Oom, and with it prosperity unequalled in the whole history of the land. Everybody was happy. There was no more unemployment. Crime ceased. The chronicler repeatedly refers to it in his memoirs as the Golden Age. And yet there remained one man on whom complete felicity had not descended. It was all right while he was actually on the Linx, but there were blank, dreary stretches of the night when King Merolchazzar lay sleepless on his couch and mourned that he had nobody to love him.

Of course, his subjects loved him in a way. A new statue had been erected in the palace square, showing him in the act of getting out of casual water. The minstrels had composed a whole cycle of up-to-date songs, commemorating his prowess with the mashie. His handicap was down to twelve. But these things are not all. A golfer needs a loving wife, to whom he can describe the day's play through the long evenings. And this was just where Merolchazzar's life was empty. No word had come from the Princess of the Outer Isles, and, as he refused to be put off with just-as-good substitutes, he remained a lonely man.

But one morning, in the early hours of a summer day, as he lay sleeping after a disturbed night, Merolchazzar was awakened by the eager hand of the Lord High Chamberlain, shaking his shoulder.

'Now what?' said the King.

'Hoots, your Majesty! Glorious news! The Princess of the Outer Isles waits without – I mean wi'oot!'

The King sprang from his couch.

'A messenger from the Princess at last!'

'Nay, sire, the Princess herself – that is to say,' said the Lord Chamberlain, who was an old man and had found it hard to accustom himself to the new tongue at his age, 'her ain sel'! And believe me, or rather, mind ah'm telling ye,' went on the honest man, joyfully, for he had been deeply exercised by his monarch's troubles, 'her Highness is the easiest thing to look at these eyes hae ever seen. And you can say I said it!'

'She is beautiful?'

'Your Majesty, she is, in the best and deepest sense of the word, a pippin!'

King Merolchazzar was groping wildly for his robes.

'Tell her to wait!' he cried. 'Go and amuse her. Ask her riddles! Tell her anecdotes! Don't let her go. Say I'll be down in a moment. Where in the name of Zoroaster is our imperial mesh-knit underwear?'

A fair and pleasing sight was the Princess of the Outer Isles as she stood on the terrace in the clear sunshine of the summer morning, looking over the King's gardens. With her delicate little nose she sniffed the fragrance of the flowers. Her blue eyes roamed over the rose bushes, and the breeze ruffled the golden curls about her temples. Presently a sound behind her caused her to turn, and she perceived a godlike man hurrying across the terrace pulling up a sock. And at the sight of him the Princess's heart sang within her like the birds down in the garden.

'Hope I haven't kept you waiting,' said Merolchazzar, apologetically. He, too, was conscious of a strange, wild exhilaration. Truly was this maiden, as his Chamberlain had said, noticeably easy on the eyes. Her beauty was as water in the desert, as fire on a frosty night, as diamonds, rubies, pearls, sapphires, and amethysts.

'Oh, no!' said the Princess, 'I've been enjoying myself. How passing beautiful are thy gardens, O King!'

'My gardens may be passing beautiful,' said Merolchazzar, earnestly, 'but they aren't half so passing beautiful as thy eyes. I have dreamed of thee by night and by day, and I will tell the world I was nowhere near it! My sluggish fancy came not within a hundred and fifty-seven miles of the reality. Now let the sun dim his face and the moon hide herself abashed. Now let the flowers bend their heads and the gazelle of the mountains confess itself a cripple. Princess, your slave!'

And King Merolchazzar, with that easy grace so characteristic of Royalty, took her hand in his and kissed it.

As he did so, he gave a start of surprise.

'By Hec!' he exclaimed. 'What hast thou been doing to thyself? Thy hand is all over little rough places inside. Has some malignant wizard laid a spell upon thee, or what is it?'

The Princess blushed.

'If I make that clear to thee,' she said, 'I shall also make clear why it was that I sent thee no message all this long while. My time was so occupied, verily I did not seem to have a moment. The fact is, these sorenesses are due to a strange, new religion to which I and my subjects have but recently become converted. And O that I might make thee also of the true faith! 'Tis a wondrous tale, my lord. Some two moons back there was brought to my Court by wandering pirates a captive of an uncouth race who dwell in the north. And this man has taught us—'

King Merolchazzar uttered a loud cry.

'By Tom, the son of Morris! Can this truly be so? What is thy handicap?'

The Princess stared at him, wide-eyed.

'Truly this is a miracle! Art thou also a worshipper of the great Gowf?'

'Am I!' cried the King. 'Am I!' He broke off. 'Listen!'

From the minstrels' room high up in the palace there came the sound of singing. The minstrels were practising a new pæan of praise – words by the Grand Vizier, music by the High Priest of Hec – which they were to render at the next full moon at the banquet of the worshippers of Gowf. The words came clear and distinct through the still air: –

'Oh, praises let us utter
To our most glorious King!
It fairly makes you stutter
To see him start his swing;
Success attend his putter!
And luck be with his drive!
And may he do each hole in two,
Although the bogey's five!'

The voices died away. There was a silence.

'If I hadn't missed a two-foot putt, I'd have done the long fifteenth in four yesterday,' said the King.

'I won the Ladies' Open Championship of the Outer Isles last week,' said the Princess.

They looked into each other's eyes for a long moment. And then, hand in hand, they walked slowly into the palace.

EPILOGUE

'Well?' we said, anxiously.

'I like it,' said the editor.

'Good egg!' we murmured.

The editor pressed a bell, a single ruby set in a fold of the tapestry upon the wall. The major-domo appeared.

'Give this man a purse of gold,' said the editor, 'and throw him out.'

P. G. Wodehouse

IN ARROW BOOKS

If you have enjoyed *The Clicking of Cuthbert*, you'll love *The Inimitable Jeeves*

FROM

The Inimitable Jeeves

'Morning, Jeeves,' I said.

'Good morning, sir,' said Jeeves.

He put the good old cup of tea softly on the table by my bed, and I took a refreshing sip. Just right, as usual. Not too hot, not too sweet, not too weak, not too strong, not too much milk, and not a drop spilled in the saucer. A most amazing cove, Jeeves. So dashed competent in every respect. I've said it before, and I'll say it again. I mean to say, take just one small instance. Every other valet I've ever had used to barge into my room in the morning while I was still asleep, causing much misery: but Jeeves seems to know when I'm awake by a sort of telepathy. He always floats in with the cup exactly two minutes after I come to life. Makes a deuce of a lot of difference to a fellow's day.

'How's the weather, Jeeves?'

'Exceptionally clement, sir.'

'Anything in the papers?'

'Some slight friction threatening in the Balkans, sir. Otherwise, nothing.'

'I say, Jeeves, a man I met at the club last night told me to put my shirt on Privateer for the two o'clock race this afternoon. How about it?'

'I should not advocate it, sir. The stable is not sanguine.'

That was enough for me. Jeeves knows. How, I couldn't say, but he knows. There was a time when I would laugh lightly, and go ahead, and lose my little all against his advice, but not now.

'Talking of shirts,' I said, 'have those mauve ones I ordered arrived yet?'

'Yes, sir. I sent them back.'

'Sent them back?'

'Yes, sir. They would not have become you.'

Well, I must say I'd thought fairly highly of those shirtings, but I bowed to superior knowledge. Weak? I don't know. Most fellows, no doubt, are all for having their valets confine their activities to creasing trousers and what not without trying to run the home; but it's different with Jeeves. Right from the first day he came to me, I have looked on him as a sort of guide, philosopher, and friend.

'Mr Little rang up on the telephone a few moments ago, sir. I informed him that you were not yet awake.'

'Did he leave a message?'

'No, sir. He mentioned that he had a matter of importance to discuss with you, but confided no details.'

'Oh, well, I expect I shall be seeing him at the club.'

'No doubt, sir.'

I wasn't what you might call in a fever of impatience. Bingo Little is a chap I was at school with, and we see a lot of each other still. He's the nephew of old Mortimer Little, who retired from business recently with a goodish pile. (You've probably heard of Little's Liniment – It Limbers Up the Legs.) Bingo biffs about London on a pretty comfortable allowance given him by his uncle, and leads on the whole a fairly unclouded life. It wasn't likely that anything which he described as a matter of importance would turn out to be really so frightfully important.

I took it that he had discovered some new brand of cigarette which he wanted me to try, or something like that, and didn't spoil my breakfast by worrying.

After breakfast I lit a cigarette and went to the open window to inspect the day. It certainly was one of the best and brightest.

'Jeeves,' I said.

'Sir?' said Jeeves. He had been clearing away the breakfast things, but at the sound of the young master's voice cheesed it courteously.

'You were absolutely right about the weather. It is a juicy morning.'

'Decidedly, sir.'

'Spring and all that.'

'Yes, sir.'

'In the spring, Jeeves, a livelier iris gleams upon the burnished dove.'

'So I have been informed, sir.'

'Right ho! Then bring me my whangee, my yellowest shoes, and the old green Homburg. I'm going into the Park to do pastoral dances.'

I don't know if you know that sort of feeling you get on these days round about the end of April and the beginning of May, when the sky's a light blue, with cotton-wool clouds, and there's a bit of a breeze blowing from the west? Kind of uplifted feeling. Romantic, if you know what I mean. I'm not much of a ladies' man, but on this particular morning it seemed to me that what I really wanted was some charming girl to buzz up and ask me to save her from assassins or something. So that it was a bit of an anti-climax when I merely ran into young Bingo Little, looking perfectly foul in a crimson satin tie decorated with horseshoes.

'Hallo, Bertie,' said Bingo.

'My God, man!' I gargled. 'The cravat! The gent's neckwear! Why? For what reason?'

'Oh, the tie?' He blushed. 'I – er – I was given it.'

He seemed embarrassed, so I dropped the subject. We toddled along a bit, and sat down on a couple of chairs by the Serpentine.

'Jeeves tells me you want to talk to me about something,' I said.

'Eh?' said Bingo, with a start. 'Oh yes, yes. Yes.'

I waited for him to unleash the topic of the day, but he didn't seem to want to get along. Conversation languished. He stared straight ahead of him in a glassy sort of manner.

'I say, Bertie,' he said, after a pause of about an hour and a quarter.

'Hallo!'

'Do you like the name Mabel?'

'No.'

'No?'

'No.'

'You don't think there's a kind of music in the word, like the wind rustling gently through the tree-tops?'

'No.'

He seemed disappointed for a moment; then cheered up.

'Of course, you wouldn't. You always were a fat-headed worm without any soul, weren't you?'

'Just as you say. Who is she? Tell me all.'

For I realized now that poor old Bingo was going through it once again. Ever since I have known him – and we were at school together – he has been perpetually falling in love with someone, generally in the spring, which seems to act on him like magic. At school he had the finest collection of actresses' photographs of anyone of his time; and at Oxford his romantic nature was a byword.

'You'd better come along and meet her at lunch,' he said, looking at his watch.

'A ripe suggestion,' I said. 'Where are you meeting her? At the Ritz?'

'Near the Ritz.'

He was geographically accurate. About fifty yards east of the Ritz there is one of those blighted tea-and-bun shops you see dotted about all over London, and into this, if you'll believe me, young Bingo dived like a homing rabbit; and before I had time to say a word we were wedged in at a table, on the brink of a silent pool of coffee left there by an early luncher.

I'm bound to say I couldn't quite follow the development of the scenario. Bingo, while not absolutely rolling in the stuff, has always had a fair amount of the ready. Apart from what he got from his uncle, I knew that he had finished up the jumping season well on the right side of the ledger. Why, then, was he lunching the girl at this God-forsaken eatery? It couldn't be because he was hard up.

Just then the waitress arrived. Rather a pretty girl.

'Aren't we going to wait—?' I started to say to Bingo, thinking it somewhat thick that, in addition to asking a girl to lunch with him in a place like this, he should fling himself on the foodstuffs before she turned up, when I caught sight of his face, and stopped.

The man was goggling. His entire map was suffused with a rich blush. He looked like the Soul's Awakening done in pink.

'Hullo, Mabel!' he said, with a sort of gulp.

'Hallo!' said the girl.

'Mabel,' said Bingo, 'this is Bertie Wooster, a pal of mine.'

'Pleased to meet you,' she said. 'Nice morning.'

'Fine,' I said.

'You see I'm wearing the tie,' said Bingo.

'It suits you beautiful,' said the girl.

Personally, if anyone had told me that a tie like that suited me, I should have risen and struck them on the mazzard, regardless of their age and sex; but poor old Bingo simply got all flustered with gratification, and smirked in the most gruesome manner.

'Well, what's it going to be today?' asked the girl, introducing the business touch into the conversation.

Bingo studied the menu devoutly.

'I'll have a cup of cocoa, cold veal and ham pie, slice of fruit cake, and a macaroon. Same for you, Bertie?'

I gazed at the man, revolted. That he could have been a pal of mine all these years and think me capable of insulting the old tum with this sort of stuff cut me to the quick.

'Or how about a bit of hot steak-pudding, with a sparkling limado to wash it down?' said Bingo.

You know, the way love can change a fellow is really frightful to contemplate. This chappie before me, who spoke in that absolutely careless way of macaroons and limado, was the man I had seen in happier days telling the head-waiter at Claridge's exactly how he wanted the chef to prepare the *sole frite au gourmet aux champignons*, and saying he would jolly well sling it back if it wasn't just right. Ghastly! Ghastly!

A roll and butter and a small coffee seemed the only things on the list that hadn't been specially prepared by the nastier-minded members of the Borgia family for people they had a particular grudge against, so I chose them, and Mabel hopped it.

'Well?' said Bingo rapturously.

I took it that he wanted my opinion of the female poisoner who had just left us.

'Very nice,' I said.

He seemed dissatisfied.

'You don't think she's the most wonderful girl you ever saw?' he said wistfully.

'Oh, absolutely!' I said, to appease the blighter. 'Where did you meet her?'

'At a subscription dance at Camberwell.'

'What on earth were you doing at a subscription dance at Camberwell?'

'Your man Jeeves asked me if I would buy a couple of tickets. It was in aid of some charity or other.'

'Jeeves? I didn't know he went in for that sort of thing.'

'Well, I suppose he has to relax a bit every now and then. Anyway, he was there, swinging a dashed efficient shoe. I hadn't meant to go at first, but I turned up for a lark. Oh, Bertie, think what I might have missed!'

'What might you have missed?' I asked, the old lemon being slightly clouded.

'Mabel, you chump. If I hadn't gone I shouldn't have met Mabel.'

'Oh, ah!'

At this point Bingo fell into a species of trance, and only came out of it to wrap himself round the pie and the macaroon.

'Bertie,' he said, 'I want your advice.'

'Carry on.'

'At least, not your advice, because that wouldn't be much good to anybody. I mean, you're a pretty consummate old ass, aren't you? Not that I want to hurt your feelings, of course.'

'No, no, I see that.'

'What I wish you would do is to put the whole thing to that fellow Jeeves of yours, and see what he suggests. You've often told me that he has helped other pals of yours out of messes. From what you tell me, he's by way of being the brains of the family.'

'He's never let me down yet.'

'Then put my case to him.'

'What case?'

'My problem.'

'What problem?'

'Why, you poor fish, my uncle, of course. What do you think my uncle's going to say to all this? If I sprang it on him cold, he'd tie himself in knots on the hearthrug.'

'One of these emotional johnnies, eh?'

'Somehow or other his mind has got to be prepared to receive the news. But how?'

'Ah!'

'That's a lot of help, that "ah"! You see, I'm pretty well dependent on the old boy. If he cut off my allowance, I should be very much in the soup. So you put the whole binge to Jeeves and see if he can't scare up a happy ending somehow. Tell him my future is in his hands, and that, if the wedding bells ring out, he can rely on me, even unto half my kingdom. Well, call it ten quid. Jeeves would exert himself with ten quid on the horizon, what?'

'Undoubtedly,' I said.

I wasn't in the least surprised at Bingo wanting to lug Jeeves into his private affairs like this. It was the first thing I would have thought of doing myself if I had been in a hole of any description. As I have frequently had occasion to observe, he is a bird of the ripest intellect, full of bright ideas. If anybody could fix things for poor old Bingo, he could.

I stated the case to him that night after dinner.

'Jeeves.'

'Sir?'

'Are you busy just now?'

'No, sir.'

'I mean, not doing anything in particular?'

'No, sir. It is my practice at this hour to read some improving book; but, if you desire my services, this can easily be postponed, or, indeed, abandoned altogether.'

'Well, I want your advice. It's about Mr Little.'

'Young Mr Little, sir, or the elder Mr Little, his uncle, who lives in Pounceby Gardens?'

Jeeves seemed to know everything. Most amazing thing. I'd been pally with Bingo practically all my life, and yet I didn't remember having heard that his uncle lived anywhere in particular.

'How did you know he lived in Pounceby Gardens?' I said.

'I am on terms of some intimacy with the elder Mr Little's cook, sir. In fact, there is an understanding.'

I'm bound to say that this gave me a bit of a start. Somehow I'd never thought of Jeeves going in for that sort of thing.

'Do you mean you're engaged?'

'It may be said to amount to that, sir.'

'Well, well!'

'She is a remarkably excellent cook, sir,' said Jeeves, as though he felt called on to give some explanation. 'What was it you wished to ask me about Mr Little?'

I sprang the details on him.

'And that's how the matter stands, Jeeves,' I said. 'I think we ought to rally round a trifle and help poor old Bingo put the thing through. Tell me about old Mr Little. What sort of a chap is he?'

'A somewhat curious character, sir. Since retiring from business he has become a great recluse, and now devotes himself almost entirely to the pleasures of the table.'

'Greedy hog, you mean?'

'I would not, perhaps, take the liberty of describing him in precisely those terms, sir. He is what is usually called a gourmet. Very particular about what he eats, and for that reason sets a high value on Miss Watson's services.'

'The cook?'

'Yes, sir.'

'Well, it looks to me as though our best plan would be to shoot young Bingo in on him after dinner one night. Melting mood, I mean to say, and all that.'

'The difficulty is, sir, that at the moment Mr Little is on a diet, owing to an attack of gout.'

'Things begin to look wobbly.'

'No, sir, I fancy that the elder Mr Little's misfortune may be turned to the younger Mr Little's advantage. I was speaking only the other day to Mr Little's valet, and he was telling me that it has become his principal duty to read to Mr Little in the evenings. If I were in your place, sir, I should send young Mr Little to read to his uncle.'

'Nephew's devotion, you mean? Old man touched by kindly action, what?'

'Partly that, sir. But I would rely more on young Mr Little's choice of literature.'

'That's no good. Jolly old Bingo has a kind face, but when it comes to literature he stops at the *Sporting Times*.'

'That difficulty may be overcome. I would be happy to select books for Mr Little to read. Perhaps I might explain my idea a little further?'

'I can't say I quite grasp it yet.'

'The method which I advocate is what, I believe, the advertisers call Direct Suggestion, sir, consisting as it does of driving an idea home by constant repetition. You may have had experience of the system?'

'You mean they keep on telling you that some soap or other is the best, and after a bit you come under the influence and charge round the corner and buy a cake?'

'Exactly, sir. The same method was the basis of all the most valuable propaganda during the recent war. I see no reason why it should not be adopted to bring about the desired result with regard to the subject's views on class distinctions. If young Mr Little were to read day after day to his uncle a series of narratives in which marriage with young persons of an inferior social status was held up as both feasible and admirable, I fancy it would prepare the elder Mr Little's mind for the reception of the information that his nephew wishes to marry a waitress in a tea-shop.'

'*Are* there any books of that sort nowadays? The only ones I ever see mentioned in the papers are about married couples who find life grey, and can't stick each other at any price.'

'Yes, sir, there are a great many, neglected by the reviewers but widely read. You have never encountered *All for Love*, by Rosie M. Banks?'

'No.'

'Nor *A Red, Red Summer Rose*, by the same author?'

'No.'

'I have an aunt, sir, who owns an almost complete set of Rosie M. Banks'. I could easily borrow as many volumes as young Mr Little might require. They make very light, attractive reading.'

'Well, it's worth trying.'

'I should certainly recommend the scheme, sir.'

'All right, then. Toddle round to your aunt's tomorrow and grab a couple of the fruitiest. We can but have a dash at it.'

'Precisely, sir.'

Also available in Arrow

The Inimitable Jeeves

P.G. Wodehouse

A Jeeves and Wooster collection

A classic collection of stories featuring some of the funniest episodes in the life of Bertie Wooster, gentleman, and Jeeves, his gentleman's gentleman – in which Bertie's terrifying Aunt Agatha stalks the pages, seeking whom she may devour, while Bertie's friend Bingo Little falls in love with seven different girls in succession (he marries the last, the bestselling romantic novelist Rosie M. Banks). And Bertie, with Jeeves's help, just evades the clutches of the terrifying Honoria Glossop . . . At its heart is one of Wodehouse's most delicious stories, 'The Great Sermon Handicap'.

arrow books

Also available in Arrow

The Heart of a Goof

P.G. Wodehouse

A Golf collection

From his favourite chair on the terrace above the ninth hole, The Oldest Member tells a series of hilarious golfing stories. From Evangeline, Bradbury Fisher's fifth wife and a notorious 'golfing giggler', to poor Rollo Podmarsh whose game was so unquestionably inept that 'he began to lose his appetite and would moan feebly at the sight of a poached egg', the game of golf, its players and their friends and enemies are here shown in all their comic glory.

arrow books

The P G Wodehouse Society (UK)

The P G Wodehouse Society (UK) was formed in 1997 to promote the enjoyment of the writings of the twentieth century's greatest humorist. The Society publishes a quarterly magazine, *Wooster Sauce*, which includes articles, features, reviews, and current Society news. Occasional special papers are also published. Society events include regular meetings in central London, cricket matches and a formal biennial dinner, along with other activities. The Society actively supports the preservation of the Berkshire pig, a rare breed, in honour of the incomparable Empress of Blandings.

MEMBERSHIP ENQUIRIES

Membership of the Society is open to applicants from all parts of the world. The cost of a year's membership in 2008 is £15. Enquiries and requests for membership forms should be made to the Membership Secretary, The P G Wodehouse Society (UK), 26 Radcliffe Rd, Croydon, Surrey, CRO 5QE, or alternatively from info@pgwodehousesociety.org.uk

The Society's website can be viewed at www.pgwodehousesociety.org.uk